C000320011

Naughty!
The Xcite Guide to Sexy Fun

Aishling Morgan

Published by Accent Press Ltd – 2009

ISBN 9781906373863

Copyright © Aishling Morgan 2009

Printed and bound in the UK

Cover Design by Red Dot Design

About the Author

Aishling Morgan is one of many pseudonyms used by the world's most prolific author of erotic literature, with over one hundred published titles. Aishling also has personal experience stretching back to the 'seventies, has been involved in London's active and vibrant fetish scene for many years, enjoys tastes that cover a multitude of pleasures and leave very few avenues unexplored, and has plenty of knowledgeable friends to help fill in the gaps. Nobody could be better qualified to write this book

Safe, Sane & Consensual

As with all good things in life, exotic sex has its drawbacks and needs to be approached with common sense. The most popular way to define what is acceptable is the phrase safe, sane and consensual, which has become a mantra among people who enjoy unconventional sex; but what does it mean?

Safe – Don't take risks with your physical health and always take precautions against sexually transmitted disease.

Sane – Be sensible, never do anything unless you are fully in control of your state of mind.

Consensual – Anything you do must be with the full consent of all parties involved.

Oh, and the law states that marks made on each other's bodies must be no more than trifling and transient, so play nice!

Introduction

This book is about pleasure; joyful, liberated, sexual pleasure, the pleasure consenting adults take in one another's bodies and minds, pleasure for its own sake, and for the friendship and love it can bring. It is also about those pleasures that go beyond what most people are used to, and beyond what is generally accepted as mainstream, not just sex, but naughty sex, the kind of sex that involves more leather than lace, more kink than kissing, that involves bound wrists and smacked bottoms, perhaps even the occasional jug full of custard.

I make no excuses and offer no apologies for the content, which is not intended to offend or to shock but to inform and delight those who are brave enough to explore their sexualities. It is my belief that each human being is unique and their sexuality no less so and that there is no right or wrong when it comes to erotic pleasures, so long as what you do is safe, sane and consensual. Sexual tastes should be celebrated, never a cause for shame or guilt, unless shame or guilt is what excites you.

If you do feel shocked, or guilty, when you open the pages of this book, please don't recoil automatically, but ask yourself why you react that way. Is it really wrong to indulge your senses, or are those feelings simply the echoes of out-dated and pointless moral values? To me, it's not wrong at all. How can it be, when it brings me so much love, and excitement, and warmth, and sheer bliss? I see naughty sex like adrenaline sport, only better. Anybody who has been abseiling or white water rafting would recognise the buzz exotic sex can bring, and that comes with the thrill of arousal and the elation of endorphin release on top, with ecstasy to cap it all. There really is nothing better.

Many people disagree, but what I must ask is that readers approach the book with an open mind and with tolerance. I enjoy everything I've described in this book, and I intend to continue to do so, because I want to extract every last ounce of spice from life. As for those out-dated and pointless moral values, they serve a purpose too, which is to provide extra spice.

> What it means:
> Top: Whoever's dishing it out.
> Bottom: Who's taking it.
> Switch: Anyone who likes both.

This is intended to be a light-hearted exploration of sexy fun, but there are serious points to be made. What this book is *not* about is coercion, making people do anything they don't want to, or do anything because they feel they have to. I do not believe in corporal punishment being inflicted on an unwilling recipient under any circumstances, nor do I support any form of enforced inequality. These things are the cultural baggage of less civilised times and should have no part in a fair and tolerant society. Nevertheless, I see no harm in using them as elements in sexual play, so long as there is understanding and consent between those involved.

After all, our background is part of who we are, and more often than not is crucial to the sort of erotic pleasure I discuss in this book, which goes far beyond the purely physical. Only the simplest forms of sexual interaction rely solely on physical sensation, and I'm not really concerned with those. What I am concerned with are those pleasures centred around the relationship between what is happening to your body and what is going on in your head.

I'm not going to pretend to understand the psychology behind sexual desire. Nobody does, and most of what has been published is either too abstruse for popular discussion, just guesswork, or tells us more about the author than it does the subject. What we can say with reasonable confidence is that each individual's desires arise from a complex mixture of nature and nurture, and

What is unthinkable to one person may be essential to another.

that therefore, while we will find common themes based both on our mutual humanity and on society, no two people will be exactly alike.

Because of this, what is unthinkable to one person may be essential to another. Neither is right, nor wrong, just different. Let's take an example, one of my favourite things – spanking. Think of being laid across another person's lap to have your bare bottom smacked, knowing that it will turn him or her on. Does it horrify you, because it seems painful, utterly inappropriate and grotesquely undignified, or does it delight you, perhaps for exactly the same reasons? Some people will react one way, other people will react the other way, or entirely differently, but the physical act is

The subtleties of sexual pleasure have more to do with the mind than with the body.

the same in every case. The difference is in your head, because the subtleties of sexual pleasure have more to do with the mind than with the body.

So, if the thought of that spanking does delight you, despite the pain and indignity or because of the pain and indignity, what should you do? Should you try and get rid of your feelings, or should you indulge them? My answer is that if you get rid of them you lose something, while if you indulge them you gain something. Why try to suppress or to destroy something which can give so much pleasure merely because it is built on what would be bad feelings were it not for the sexual arousal they provide? Far better, surely, to accept your feelings for what they are. If you want to do it, don't make it a problem, make it a pleasure. The same goes for every other subject I cover in this book.

Knowledge can make the difference between an unpleasant experience that is only likely to put you off and an introduction to what may become a lifelong passion.

If the thought of that spanking delights you anyway, and perhaps doesn't seem to have anything to do with pain or indignity, then good for you. On the other hand, if it seems pointless, incomprehensible, or just plain silly, but you've never tried it, then I suggest you give it a go. The physical side alone can be wonderful, although you'll be missing out on the full potential of the experience, just as an atheist can never fully appreciate the magnificence of a great cathedral. However, read this book first, and make sure your partner has read it as well.

That's because if you are going to be the top, i.e. the one doing the spanking or tying somebody up or simply pouring a large can of spaghetti hoops down his or her knickers, it is important to know what you're doing. It may sound simple, and it's not rocket science, but there is a great deal to know, and that knowledge can make the difference between an unpleasant experience that is only likely to put you off and an introduction to what may become a lifelong passion.

I would go further, and argue that if you are going to dish it out you ought to know how it feels to be on the receiving end. To me, it seems self evident that the more experience you have of a sensation the better you will be able to understand it, even if you lack the desire and so can never fully understand. Many people disagree, and argue that the purest experience can only be achieved by each person remaining in his or her preferred role, giving or receiving. Others enjoy both roles equally, myself included, which I feel is an important qualification when it comes to giving advice.

This is a practical guide, dealing with what to do rather than how to go about finding somebody to do it with, so I'm not going to discuss relationships in depth and the focus is always on what people can do together. It's meant to be for everybody, but

Edge Play: Any risky or very intense practice, generally beyond the scope of this book.

I'm not going to go into every possible permutation of male, female, gay, straight and in-between for every activity. More often than not, if you can do it with a man, you can do it with a woman too, while the exceptions are generally a matter of common sense. Most of those who volunteered to model for me were female so the majority of the photographs used to illustrate different practices are of women, not because I feel these practices are more appropriate for women, but for the sake of convenience. I would also like to point out that with the exception of a few stock shots all the pictures are of genuine enthusiasts and were either donated by friends, taken on a time-for-prints basis or, most often, simply done for the fun of it.

On the writing front, those who like more defined roles will have to excuse me if I seem to assume that everybody is bisexual, polyamorous and happy to be both giving and receiving. It's just easier that way, honest!

Anyway, while most people will see exotic sex as the icing on the cake, for many it's the main attraction, or something entirely separate. Penetrative sex need not always be your goal. That way, if you're unattached, or in an open relationship, you can have as many partners as you like, indulge mutual pleasures with friends and expand the horizons of your sexuality far beyond what most people experience. You can also extend the experience. Conventional sex rarely lasts a full hour, more refined variations such as tantric sex perhaps a few hours, but an afternoon of pony-girl play followed by an intimate party and then bed can mean twelve hours or more of gradually rising erotic pleasure before reaching climax.

So have fun ...

Safe Words

A safe word is a word used to stop play.

Safe words are an essential part of any form of sex play in which one person has control over another or in which strong mental or physical sensations are involved. The safe word should be chosen beforehand, and all parties involved should agree on it and be prepared to stop what they are doing if anybody uses that word. In order to prevent confusion the word should be something unexpected in the context of what you're doing, because you may well want to beg for mercy in the full knowledge that it will be denied, but you're unlikely to say "hippopotamus" at random while having wax dripped on your bare bottom.

A common choice is the traffic light code: "Red" for stop immediately, "Amber" for slow down, and "Green" for start again. If you are unable to speak, perhaps when you've had your face pushed into a chocolate gateau, it can help to have a sign as well, such as slapping the palm of your hand down on a flat surface in the traditional wrestlers' gesture of submission.

There are four main reasons why somebody might need to use a safe word:

Accidental: When something has gone wrong; such as a piece of rope tied too tight, your glasses falling off, or a dozen large policemen having walked into the club.

Physical: When the situation has become painful for you or is about to go further than you're happy with; for example, being laid bare bottom in a public place.

7

Emotional: When you hit a mental boundary; this can be unexpected, extremely intense and is no less important than physical problems.

Social: When the situation is wrong; perhaps if you enjoy having an audience but somebody you're not comfortable with asks to join in.

This may seem obvious, but play will be a lot better if you don't have to keep checking that everything is all right. A safe word also gives you the opportunity to break role, negotiate or sort things out and then start again. Use it when *you* need it, and don't worry about people thinking you're a wimp or no fun. If you'd like to go further, you can always come back to it another time.

For the top, you're in charge, so make sure everybody involved knows what the safe word is and respects it immediately when used. Never assume that you know better than the person who is on the receiving end. If you feel he or she could have taken more, discuss it afterwards. Never ignore a safe word.

Who's the Boss?

Domination & Submission

Do you like to go on top? If you do, then you probably have the makings of a top or dominant, somebody who likes to be in control during sex. If you prefer going underneath, then you probably have the makings of a bottom or submissive. If you like it every which way, then you probably have the makings of a switch, who enjoys both domination and submission.

> Power Exchange – Where one partner willingly gives up control to the other in order to enhance a sexual experience.

That's really all there is to it, although if you get into it at all deeply you'll find there are plenty of subtle distinctions, not always easily defined. It's also important to remember that you can enjoy all sorts of kinky sex without getting involved in domination and submission at all.

Tabloid newspapers love to paint domination and submission as bizarre, even sinister, and definitely shameful. Maybe that sells papers, but it's an attitude which belongs with petticoats on piano legs. Domination and submission is ingrained in our psyche, going back long before we were human. OK, so we've moved on a bit since the days of grunting alpha males and female troop hierarchy, or at least I'd like to think so, but why not have fun with it anyway?

The key is power exchange, where one partner willingly gives up control to the other in order to enhance a sexual experience. This may be something as simple as polishing your partner's boots, which becomes a significant act of submission. Just about everybody does it on some level, even if it's just a

> The fact that somebody enjoys submissive sex does not mean they are sexually available to anybody and everybody.

question of who has the stronger personality, or even whose needs are stronger at that specific instant. Once this is accepted, you open up a whole world of pleasures, which can be as simple as taking turns to

> Just because you like to defer to your partner in bed doesn't make you inferior.

obey each other's commands, or as deep and as complicated as you please. The important thing to remember is that you are equal at heart, that just because you like to defer to your partner in bed doesn't make you inferior, or mean that you don't deserve respect. In practice, many people in senior, responsible positions enjoy taking a submissive role in bed, often because it's an excellent way of shedding the stresses and cares of working life.

Enjoying submissive sex doesn't necessarily mean relinquishing control. I recall one girl at a party who had the undivided attention of six men; four to hold her down, one to pull her hair and one to smack her bottom, but all doing exactly as they were told. That's called "topping from the bottom", and is frowned upon by many but to me is simply one more facet in the complex world of sexual play.

Not that a dominance and submission (D/s) relationship necessarily has to be sexual, at least not in the conventional sense. Strictly speaking, there doesn't even have to be physical contact. Usually there will be both, but it may be that for you dominance

> Subspace – The deep feeling of euphoria that comes with the best submissive sexual experiences.

and submission works best as foreplay, with your roles abandoned once things get sufficiently steamy, or as a tease, with the roles reversed once the submissive can't take it any more. Any combination is possible, because there are no rules except those you make yourselves.

Negotiation

For dominance and submission to work in a relationship it is essential that everybody gets what they want, not just the dominant partner, and no two individuals are going to be 100% compatible. That means you're going to need to negotiate and probably lay down some ground rules.

Hard Limit – A point beyond which you are not prepared to go or a practice you find unacceptable.

Some people will be content to derive their pleasure solely from fulfilling their partner's desires, but this is rare. La Marquise, perhaps the most dedicated and experienced dominant woman I have met, has found only three men capable of meeting her needs out of hundreds of hopeful candidates.

More often, you'll both want to express your fantasies, which won't be fully compatible, so you'll need to compromise. Communication is essential. Define your desires and boundaries, what you're willing to do and where your hard limits lie, but always with the awareness that people change over time. Consent is not something that can be given unconditionally and permanently, but exists

To deny somebody the right to withdraw their consent is abuse. No excuses. No ifs. No buts. It's abuse.

from day to day and from moment to moment. To deny somebody the right to withdraw his or her consent is

12

abuse. No excuses. No ifs. No buts. It's abuse. You must be prepared to renegotiate, whether it relates to your relationship or just what's happening at that moment, although, in practice, once you've been together for any length of time you're sure to know each other well enough and be able to read each other well enough that it's seldom necessary to discuss how you interact.

> Your roles may extend beyond the bedroom, but don't take unfair advantage of your dominance.

You may find that your roles expand beyond the bedroom, but don't push your luck. If you use your dominance to skive out of your share of the washing up, and that's not arousing for your partner, it's probably going to cause problems with your relationship. So don't lose sight of what it's all about – pleasure and fulfilment. Some people need to maintain their roles all the time, what is known as a 24/7 D/s relationship, but that does not remove the need for negotiation.

Contracts

You may want to put your agreement in writing, perhaps so that you can refer to it when needed, or perhaps because it gives you pleasure to do so. This can be done as a serious document, setting out each of your privileges and responsibilities, or with an element of fantasy, stating how you would like your relationship to work in an ideal world. The details of your contract are entirely personal, but might, for example, give the dominant partner the right to punish the submissive partner whenever it seems appropriate, but balanced by the responsibilities of not

doing so without good reason and for providing comfort afterwards.

A contract can provide a useful framework for a D/s relationship, and also a great deal of pleasure for both partners. What it can never be is legally binding, and what it should never be is immutable. If you are the dominant partner in such a relationship, you have the responsibility of looking after the submissive, even if his or her greatest desire is to be used as your sex toy, and so you must always be prepared to change the rules if they're not working. Refuse and you've probably just put the first crack in your relationship.

Collaring

We usually acknowledge a close bond to another person with a ring, but as the submissive partner in a D/s relationship you might well prefer to wear a collar, which is a much more potent symbol of your status. This can be as simple as a gold chain or a velvet choker, which is useful if you want to wear it permanently but don't want other people to realise what it signifies, or if you have a sensitive job. Otherwise you might prefer something with stronger symbolism, a plait of rope or leather, a steel chain or torque – which are

> A collar makes a potent symbol of your status as the submissive partner.

available in beautiful designs – or a full-sized leather collar (like the one illustrated), perhaps with a padlock. It's easy to make your own, and you may feel that's the

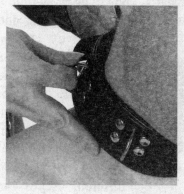

only way it carries any significance, but there are some beautiful collars available both from ordinary jewellers and specialists.

Putting on your collar for the first time can be a very important moment and some people make this into a ceremony, either between those involved or with witnesses and friends so that it becomes something like a common law marriage. Usually it is the dominant partner who collars the submissive, but a collar does not necessarily imply submission, or, if you switch, you might both like to collar the other. Again, there are no rules except those you make yourselves and, so long as you respect each other's right to consent, nobody has the right to tell you how you should or shouldn't run your relationship.

Switching

It may be that you take a more playful, less serious attitude to domination and submission, or that you enjoy both, equally or otherwise. Or it may be that you need both with the same intensity that other people need one or the

The idea that people who switch are merely undecided is a myth born of a lack of understanding.

other, or that you prefer to choose dominance or submission as the outcome of a physical contest, or a mental one.

In any case, you are what's known as a switch – somebody who takes pleasures in both dominant and submissive roles.  You may still have a preference for one role or the other, or it may be that you respond to different people in different ways, even people of different sexes in different ways, as a woman might enjoy dominating other women but submitting to men, or *vice versa*. It may be that your preferences change with time, or with your mood, or you may be capable of altering your perspective in a matter of moments, even of indulging in both at the same time. Whatever the case may be, your sexuality is no less valid. The idea that people who switch are merely undecided is a myth born of a lack of understanding, much like the idea that bisexual people are merely undecided. If it's in your head, it makes perfect sense, but if it's not you can never fully understand it. To read some of the literature on the subject, you would think that the roles are immutable, but in my experience more people switch than don't, especially among those who enjoy multiple partners. Some are happy to switch for anyone they're happy to play with, for others it's only occasionally and with particular partners, and I've known plenty of people never even admit that they switch except

In my experience, more people switch than don't.

16

to a few close friends.

Taken a step further, you may find the whole idea of one person leading your sex play to be limiting, even stifling, and so prefer to indulge in exactly the same things on an equal basis, each doing whatever is appropriate for the moment.

The obvious advantage of switching is that you get the best of both worlds, although those who don't can argue that you never fully experience either. Having played with many people over many years, and watched many more, my opinion is that experiences are no less intense for switches, and that exchanging roles gives an added dimension to your pleasure. Another advantage is that you can gain a better understanding of how your partner feels, both physically and emotionally, because you have first-hand knowledge of those same feelings. Be careful though, because people's responses are so individual that you may assume you know how your partner feels when in fact his or her personal reaction is very different from your own.

> You may find the whole idea of one person leading your sex play to be limiting.

If you and your partner both switch there are inevitably going to be moments when you both want to take the same role. For many this can be settled by a quick wrestling match, but that has the disadvantage that the stronger or more skilled partner is usually going to win. Playing a game of chance is fairer, can add a thrilling element of apprehension to the situation and can lead to a really excellent scene as you take revenge on each other. Revenge, in a playful sense, is often an

> To understand a physical sensation is one thing, but never assume you know exactly how your partner feels.

important concept to switches, and can add a great deal of spice to your sex life by providing an added motivation

> Revenge, in a playful sense, is often an important concept to switches.

not only to get down to it but to explore new possibilities.

Difficulties are almost certain to arise in any power exchange relationship in which one partner wants to switch but the other does not, and for many people switching simply does not work. This can sometimes be solved by involving other people, but if that's unacceptable you can only do your best to negotiate a compromise. It may well be that in order for your sex life to work at all the switch partner needs to try and suppress his or her incompatible feelings, and that may work, but those feelings are very unlikely to disappear.

Cuckolding

Cuckolding is where swinging meets domination and submission. The submissive partner, almost always a man in this case, enjoys the dominant partner having sex with other people, male or female. He may prefer to be excluded completely, but more often will want to watch, perhaps serve his partner and her lover, even join in, but strictly in a subservient role. A classic cuckolding scenario is for a man to be available for oral sex

> Bull: A dominant, male third party in a cuckolding relationship.

while his partner enjoys another man, not only licking her, but sucking her bull's cock.

18

Accepting your own needs

It's not always easy to accept your sexuality, especially if it goes against what is expected of you by society and family. The last 50 years have seen extraordinary changes in social attitudes to sex, perhaps most notably in tolerance of homosexuality as until 1967 any sexual interaction between men was a criminal offence. Now we are moving towards full equality, yet many people still find it difficult to accept their own gender preferences, never mind express them openly. The same is true for kinky sex, and especially dominance and submission.

Society presents us with desirable gender images – the successful career woman, the man in touch with his feminine side – which may go against your desires. If you have the courage to express socially unacceptable desires you will sometimes encounter hostility, perhaps merely shock and misunderstanding, but very possibly physical assault. Unfortunately, while the UK government recognises most forms of discrimination and is ready to legislate against them, this only goes so far for sexuality.

Because of this you do need to be careful, which is a shame, but please don't allow yourself to be kept down. Now that we have the internet, it is easy to find like-minded people, whatever you're into, and without risking the social disapprobation that can still ruin careers. So make your own moral judgements rather than allowing society to impose them on you. Ask yourself: is what I want to do safe, sane and consensual? If it is, go ahead and do it.

Putting on a
Show

Fetishism & Erotic Display

The basis of erotic display is the effect of the human body on the human mind. At its simplest, this is the visual element of the same attraction that compels animals to mate. Just as a female cat will lift her haunches and roll on her back to show that she is ready, so a female human will dress to accentuate her breasts, bottom and belly, essentially for the same purpose. Admittedly, human behaviour is a little more complicated than that, with the need for warmth, social expectations, conspicuous consumption and other factors all affecting the way we dress, but I'm only concerned with the sexual aspects, and even then only as they relate to fetishism. Not that it's easy to draw a dividing line between what is fetishistic and what is not. It's possible to have a fetish for any part of the body, overtly sexual or otherwise, and for any object.

> You can have a fetish for any part of the body or any object.

Even as commonplace an item as a gent's tie can have fetishistic appeal, just as a gent's suit is in many ways the archetype

of dominant male imagery.

Jeans make a good example. They have a long history and have been a popular fetish since the 50s, both sexually and as part of US culture. Originally, jeans were a tough garment designed for work. They were worn by both men and women in US factories during World War

II, but gradually became associated with both youth and rebellion, giving them a strong sexual charge. It is no accident that James Dean wears jeans in *Rebel Without a Cause*, nor the way some of the posters emphasise his buttocks and crotch, while on the female side who can doubt the eroticism of the way Marilyn Monroe's bottom fills out her jeans in *River of No Return*?

> To be a fetish, a desire must be strong – an irrational reverence.

Jeans have played an essential part in fashion and therefore in erotic display ever since, with their cultural background and visual appeal making them ideal material for the potential fetishist. Not that merely admiring a well filled pair of jeans makes you a fetishist. The desire has to be strong, what the Shorter Oxford English Dictionary calls an "irrational reverence".

The same has been true of male military trousers and female corsetry in the 19th century, stockings in the 20th, sailor suits in Japan, bull-fighting costume in Spain, and so on. In each case, a garment has become fetishised, as none of those garments were originally intended to be sexually provocative.

So it's not all about leather thigh boots and rubber shorts, although those play their part. In fact, if a look or a material or an object exists, it can be fetishised and probably has been. When it comes to sexual taste, there's no such thing as good or bad, only what works for the individual. In the case of jeans their sexual appeal is obvious, but that is by no

> A fetish is there to be expressed, sexually, so fetishistic imagery has come to drive the way people dress for kinky sex.

means always the case. Shoes are one step removed, because while they may enhance the wearer's appearance and send out all sorts of complex and subtle social signals, they are not overtly sexual. Yet shoe fetishism is extremely common and takes many forms aside from the typical image of male obsession with female thigh boots or high heels. Army boots or heavy work boots exert a fetishistic fascination for many, especially

Riding boots are another common object of adoration, wellies rather less so.

among gay men, but also lesbian women. Riding boots are another common object of adoration, wellies rather less so, but even sandals have their devotees.

In other cases, a fetish can be purely psychological, or completely removed from ordinary sexual experience, and, as such, may seem meaningless or ridiculous to other people. Clowns, anybody? Wool? Satsumas? I've known all three.

OK, so my satsuma fetishist friend didn't actually want to dress as a satsuma, but the principle is the same. A fetish is there to be expressed, sexually, so fetishistic imagery has come to drive the way people dress for kinky sex, either to satisfy a personal fetish, or to express a fetish for other peoples' pleasure, often a popular cultural fetish.

Go to any kinky club and you'll see fetishistic clothing on every side, but only a small proportion of those who wear it will be actually fetishists. Most will have a milder sexual interest, simply enjoying the look, or wanting to dress to impress, or it may be all about fashion. The picture above shows Joanna in the Barnet Bastille, in what is not only a classic look but fits perfectly with her surroundings. She is dressed almost completely in leather, and would certainly appeal to a leather fetishist, but that does not necessarily mean she has a leather fetish herself.

Reading the signals somebody else is sending out is both important and tricky.

What you can guarantee is that the further their look is from what's acceptable to the mainstream, the more likely the wearers are to be serious fetishists, or at least to have deliberately chosen a look that carries erotic power for them or their partner. The guy leaning on the bar in biker gear and shades may or may not be a leather fetishist. He may only be dressed that way so that he can pass the dress code, but the girl wearing nothing but a little rubber snout and a curly pink tail is very aware of how she looks, and it's important to her.

What it means to her is another matter, which is why reading the signals somebody else is sending out is both important and tricky. In the above example, the girl might have a fetish for being a piggy-girl – something we'll come to later – or she might be a submissive dressed that way to please her top, or as a punishment. What matters is that it brings her pleasure and excitement, just as your own choices do for you. As always, tolerance is essential, and if you

What matters is that is brings pleasure and excitement.

find her interesting, so is tact. Never put down the way somebody else chooses to express themselves, even if it does seem ridiculous to you.

Tact and mutual acceptance of each others' choices can make a kinky club a wonderfully inclusive and accepting place, especially if you've felt you were alone with your unusual desires for any length of time. At a typical club, there will be people in leather and rubber, in fabulously exotic costumes or near naked, cross-dressed or expressing iconic male or female imagery, maybe in a cassock, in harness, or any one of dozens of other costumes.

Nor is fetishistic imagery only for the "beautiful people"; far from it. Whatever your body shape there will be a niche for you, while those who are into kinky sex tend to be more versatile in their tastes and less heavily influenced by media imagery of what is 'acceptable'. After all, if you're a man whose driving sexual need is to be pinned helpless beneath a dominant woman, then the heavier she is the better, while for her she is able to delight in her physical power in a way that would be impossible in mainstream society.

So how to dress? If you are a fetishist you'll already know and it's just a question of getting the best out of what's available. If your interest is mainly in domination and submission you may prefer to adopt the classic  imagery: fully clad and black for the top, naked or near naked for the bottom. Otherwise, there is plenty of choice, and my own feeling is that it's best to find a balance between your personal tastes and your body image.

Perhaps you don't fit the stereotypical image of a dominatrix? Dress up as an old fashioned matron and the boys will flock to you, especially the ones who like to be spanked.

Costume play

Plenty of people dress up in costume in order to spice up their sex lives, and plenty of people focus on particular costumes, sometimes for the sake of a fetish, sometimes not. All the most popular examples are dealt with individually below, but the basic idea is the same: to use costume to create an erotic image. What we wear sends signals to other people about who we are, regardless of choice and whether we like it or not, so by choosing particular clothes for sex you're making a statement both about who you are and how you'd like to be perceived. This can be done very easily.

The three pictures show the same scene but two things change – her pose and the prop she is using. They quite clearly belong to the same set, but, taken separately, they project very different images. The first is a simple nude pose, without any specific implications. In the second, she

It's impossible to draw a line between what is sexy and what's not.

has become a college girl caught sunbathing in the nude and trying to cover her modesty with one arm and her boater. The third is similar, but her riding hat and sassy attitude makes her stronger and the appeal of the scene is changed. Or perhaps your interpretation is entirely different, which goes to show an image's meaning is in the eye of the beholder, and that what you perceive is not necessarily what was intended.

A good example of perceived image is cosplay, which is spreading rapidly from where it originated in the Far East. Cosplay is by no means always sexual, but there is a strong erotic element to it, with fans dressing up as characters from anime art or their favourite comics, often in colourful wigs and wonderfully kinky outfits. There is immense variation, but the styles are united by deliberate exaggeration and a focus on sexual imagery, which may seem straightforward, but to fully understand it you need at least a grounding in Japanese contemporary culture and comic art. An overlapping craze, mainly North American at present, is to dress up as a favourite cartoon animal – a furry. Their outfits are less often designed with sex in mind, but the most popular choices usually have an erotic edge; a fox or cat rather than an armadillo or a porcupine. Is it erotic? Is it not? The answer is neither "yes" nor "no", but lies in the mind of the individual.

All this shows that it's impossible to draw an objective line between what's sexy and what's not, as it's such an individual thing, but as far as fetish erotica is concerned, there are certain firm favourites. Many of the strongest and most popular images fit into one of four groups – female and dominant, female and submissive, male and dominant, male and submissive – although fetishism doesn't necessarily have anything to do with domination or submission, any more so than more general erotic display.

Female Dominant

Perhaps the two words which best sum up the archetypal of the dominant woman are beauty and denial. The traditional image of the dominant female in fetish gear is a leather or rubber body suit, thigh boots and a whip, which certainly looks beautiful but is as much the product of submissive male fantasy as it is what dominant women actually like to wear. Yet a body suit does achieve what is essential to many dominant women – to display the contours of her body without revealing more than she wishes. A thin, tight layer of material hints at what is beneath without actually exposing anything, allowing her to tease her admirers while remaining firmly in control. The same is true of high boots, gloves, coats and veils, all of which impose a barrier between her body and his eyes, a barrier she can adjust at will, withholding or granting her favour as she pleases.

La Marquise's outfit in the picture is a classic illustration; beautiful, elegant, designed to emphasise her femininity while allowing her precise control over what she reveals. Both her dress and corset are fine silk, adding an opulence to her look, something which also sits well with dominant female imagery. Whatever she wears, it will always be stylish, well fitted and made of high quality materials.

What might seem surprising is how restrictive some of this clothing is; corsets, hobble skirts and exaggeratedly high heels for example, but remember that these garments restrict access as much as they restrict movement, while a dominant women doesn't need freedom of movement because she has other people to do things for her.

If you do find restriction irritating, there are plenty of other choices, while it's

> You need that vital spark within you to carry off the image.

important to remember that ultimately it's not the clothes that make the woman. No matter how you dress, you need that vital spark within you to carry off the image, and a woman with enough presence and self-confidence can be quite capable of dominating a scene even when she's stark naked. That would be the exception, but it is possible to use accessories to accentuate your dominance while wearing very little else; for example, a combination of boots, gloves, a peaked cap and a whip, perhaps with a bikini or some pretty underwear if you feel so inclined.

Alternatively, you might want to draw from authoritative imagery, whether female or male, and not necessarily modern, accentuating the look for best effect. Classic examples include the governess or school ma'am, traditionally armed with a cane; formal riding gear complete with a whip and perhaps even spurs; police or military, a matron or senior nurse. A male business suit gives a striking image, or you can go for raw power, a touch of cruelty, whatever appeals. It's also a good idea to choose carefully; your boyfriend might be on his knees in seconds to you as a police inspector, but his reaction might be very different to a traffic warden's uniform.

Female Submissive

If the essence of dominant female imagery is not to reveal too much, then the reverse is true for submissive female imagery, which is designed to enhance a woman's availability. However, eager males would do well to note that this does not mean she is necessarily available to them personally, often just the opposite. What matters is her sense of exposure, her display of a yielding, sexual, archetypal feminine nature, which generally means having plenty of flesh on show or easily laid bare. Yet even full nudity is not inherently submissive.

Submission, no less than dominance, is something that comes from within. The picture shows Leia-Ann Woods in her retro-style evening finery. Another woman dressed the same way might well come across as dominant, but Leia-Ann's pose could not possibly be taken for anything but submissive and goes with her nature.

So you don't need to be stark naked and walking on a lead with a rosy bottom, unless that's your style. Any sort of gentle image can work to good effect, also anything generally associated with obeying others or being junior in some way. Not that a submissive image necessarily means you're going to do as you're told. After all, probably the most popular submissive female image of all is a college girl in uniform, which is more often associated with a sassy attitude than with being well behaved. Don't let anybody tell you otherwise, either, because how you express yourself is a personal thing and enjoying submissive sex does not mean you have to be a doormat, by any means.

Aside from the ever popular college girl look, maid's or nurse's uniforms work well, as do junior ranks in the police or military, which are always good choices if you're not comfortable being nude or near nude. Pretty underwear is always an option, and doesn't necessarily have to be modern. In fact, period underwear is so popular and so striking it needs its own sections, below. Being partially in bondage sends a strong signal, even if your movement isn't restricted, also harnesses, pony-girl gear and so on, all of which we'll look at in detail later. The sort of clothing that's generally associated with commercial sex can work, along with almost anything in pink or very short, but can also send out mixed signals and it's important to distinguish between what's sexual and submissive and what's just sexual.

Male Dominant

Men tend to be the more visual sex, and women seeking dominant men are far more attracted by what's going on in his head than they are by his appearance, so when it comes to looking the part you might well be excused for thinking you needn't bother. If you're the real deal, the first thing that comes to hand will do just fine, and if

31

you're not, then no mere look is going to help you. In practice, you may find that shuffling around in your underpants and a pair of carpet slippers fails to spark her ardour.

In the picture, Trainer Bryan of the North Downs Pony Club (and that has nothing to do with horses) probably wouldn't even get past the door of a fetish club, but there's no doubting the dominance of his look.

Ours has been, and to an extent still is, a male dominated society, so there's a strong link between what we think of as a dominant image and the image of a successful male. A suit and tie, if smart enough, may be all you need, especially if you don't normally dress that way or mix with others who do. Taken a step further, faultless evening dress can be very effective indeed. If you do normally wear a suit and tie, then a rougher look is more likely to work; leathers for instance, or any strong alternative culture image.

The stereotypical male dominant image, and one you'll see a lot at clubs, is black leather trousers, jacket and maybe a waistcoat, heavy boots and a white shirt, often accompanied by a beard. Army gear is also effective, as it is both a casual, mercenary look and smart uniform, but my feeling is that what really matters is giving an impression of being strong and capable, preferably both mentally and physically, because the

32

essence of male dominance is to be able to provide support and protection.

Male authority, and the right to punish that goes with it, can also be erotic for many women, so that when in a more playful situation, outfits such as an old fashioned master's gown and mortarboard work well, especially if you're armed with a cane or perhaps a strap. This also means that less conventional authority images work well, so if you're a big fat man try dressing up as Father Christmas for a club and you might find you're surprisingly popular.

Oh, and don't wear trainers.

Male Submissive

Social conventions don't allow much scope for the expression of male sexual submission, which is perhaps  why so much of the imagery is borrowed from women, although not all by any means. Many men prefer full nudity, or to wear as little as the situation allows them to get away with; perhaps just a pair of tight briefs or shorts, usually in clinging material and often leather or rubber. College uniform works for some, often in an old fashioned style, but other uniforms are relatively rare.

Complete leather or rubber outfits designed to convey a submissive look can be bought, but it's an expensive taste. A collar and lead conveys the same message, as do wrist cuffs and body harness, all of which are cheaper and easier to make for yourself. If you're single and thinking of going out on the club scene, be aware that there's a lot of competition and you need to stand out, and that it can be tricky to find the right balance between expressing your own needs and finding a mate. Women

> Women often prefer a man to be dressed, and for his submission to come from within or be expressed in his behaviour.

often prefer a man to be dressed anyway, and for their submission to come from within or be expressed in their behaviour, as Mark shows in the picture.

Then there's cross-dressing, which is too big a subject to go into in any real detail but which definitely deserves a mention. A desire to cross-dress doesn't necessarily mean a man is sexually submissive, and it definitely doesn't mean that he is gay, although this is a common misconception. Nevertheless, many sexually submissive men and gay, bisexual or bi-curious men do like to cross-dress and for a wide variety of often highly individual reasons. For example, there is cross-dressing purely for the sake of being in female clothes, often called pinaforing, and cross-dressing for the sake of pleasure through humiliation, often called petticoating.

In both cases, the image is not so much an imitation of feminine dress, but an exaggeration, even a parody. Women sometimes feel this is insulting, particularly with petticoating, because it shouldn't be humiliating for a man to be made to dress like the object of his adoration, but, in practice, he knows that he is quite incapable of imitating her successfully and can only ever achieve a ridiculous and grotesque pastiche of her beauty. After all, a submissive man in frilly panties does not look like a girl; he looks like a man in frilly panties and that is the source of his pleasure. If that's your thing, then you are by no means alone, as there is a small industry dedicated to flounces and frills, to pleated skirts and frilly panties, all of which go together to create what's known as the sissy look.

Cross-dressing

Plenty of people cross-dress without wanting to express a dominant or submissive sexuality, mainly men, but also women. This may be in order to express gay male or lesbian sexuality, because they take pleasure in a sense of transgression and mischief, for the feel of different

materials on their skin, or to enjoy aspects of sexual display that are only socially acceptable to the opposite sex.

It's normal for human societies to have customs or even rules about how men and women should and should not dress. Ours is no different except that in recent times it has become largely acceptable for women to adopt what was previously exclusively male costume. Ivy could walk down the high street of any town in Britain as she is shown in the photo and not draw adverse attention, even with her pencilled in beard and moustache, yet any man in equivalent female costume is going to be the subject of disapproving looks at the very least. That in itself demonstrates how meaningless the taboo against cross-dressing is, and nobody should feel ashamed for enjoying it as a fetish, or for any other reason. Fortunately, it is not something that has been legislated against.

There are now specialist suppliers to cater for crossdressers, although the focus is almost entirely on men. Feminine shoes are available in large sizes, along with the exaggerated styles that are often popular with crossdressers but almost never worn by women. Otherwise, a sewing machine and a little courage at the lingerie counter is all you need to put together any outfit your imagination can conceive.

Burlesque

One popular fashion with a strong element of fetish is burlesque. This began as theatrical parody designed to mock the pompous and the pretentious but fell out of fashion with the decline of music halls and popular theatre. There was always a sexual element to it, but this is much more pronounced in the recent revival embodied by Ditta von Teese.

Most burlesque imagery is feminine, whether it be for women or for male crossdressers, and even ultra-feminine, designed to emphasise curves and reveal just as much as the wearer wishes. It is also retrospective, drawing on historical imagery, whether erotic or not, and giving it a new, sexy edge. Stockings, corsetry and old-fashioned lingerie are all popular, also high heels, buckles and buttons, ribbons and lace, feathers, perhaps mixed in with modern elements to create a striking and highly erotic look.

The picture shows Ivy in the middle of a burlesque striptease routine. Her outfit came from as many different shops as she has items of clothing left on. Tease is always an important element of burlesque, with plenty hinted at but not necessarily revealed, again reflecting at historical attitudes to nudity. This can be great fun as a fetish look and in the bedroom, although, unless you tie him down, you're not likely to get very far into the teasing part.

> Buying burlesque gear can simply be a matter of making imaginative use of everyday clothing.

There is enough overlap between fetish and burlesque to make it acceptable club wear, while its mainstream popularity makes it easier to get away with than many other styles. Buying burlesque gear can simply be a matter of making imaginative use of everyday clothing, but if you want something a little more exotic, such as a scarlet top hat, there are plenty of specialist shops. London's Brick Lane area is particularly good.

Historical Erotica

Sexy outfits based on old-fashioned clothing were popular long before the revival of burlesque. They can be drawn from any period and any culture; perhaps Ancient Egypt or Rome, even the Stone Age if a fur loincloth does it for you. Two periods from our own culture are particularly popular for the fetish look, late Victorian and post WWII. Both were periods of striking imagery and also of concealment, adding mystery to their erotic appeal.

Clothing has never been more elaborate that in Western culture between the middle of the 19th century and WWI. Crinolines, bustles, bloomers, split-seam and panel-back drawers all date from that era, while it was also the heyday of the corset. The male look also has potential, with formal black suits, walking canes, even stovepipe hats, but may be a bit of a specialist taste. Full female dress is also strictly for the true fan, but female undergarments are a different matter.

Corsets are now so popular that they deserve their own section, but chemises, drawers and combinations (chemise and drawers together as one garment) are all quite rare but have a wonderfully saucy look and feel all of their own. Bras didn't come in until the corset started to go out of

fashion, and the chemise was worn beneath a corset to provide comfort and a little support. Usually made from silk of lightweight cotton, they most definitely were not made to be seen, which makes them all the more enchanting when they are. Drawers are saucier still. A corset and heavy skirts made it impractical for a woman to take down her underwear, so drawers were designed either as "splitters", which have an open seam at the back, usually hidden among voluminous folds but easily opened, as in the picture, or with buttons holding a panel of material in place. Petticoats are also very sweet, and a typical Victorian lady would have worn three; an inner one of cotton for cleanliness, a middle one of flannel for warmth and an outer one of taffeta to rustle as she moved. All three would have been heavily trimmed, as would the chemise and drawers, although the highly extravagant lace trim you often see in smutty pictures of the period was probably more typical of Parisian brothels than the respectable wardrobe. The girl in the picture has discarded her dress, corset and chemise, but has her petticoats turned up and her splitters open. She also has knee length woollen stockings and square-heeled leather shoes. I think we can assume that the rose was not an everyday accessory.

> Seamed stockings have a particular appeal to many people, sometimes to the point of obsession.

Even more popular is the look borrowed from the late 40s and the 50s, often associated with the model Bettie Page, with elegant dresses and full cut undergarments that give plenty of support and also conceal as much as they reveal; girdles and suspenders, full cut bras and panties. Seamed stockings have a particular appeal to many people, sometimes to the point of obsession. The big advantage of this period is that it's possible to buy most garments, either as modern reproductions or originals.

Underwear from the 20s and 30s can be just as pretty, short cut, split seam knickers for example, but is harder to get hold off. Anything from the 60s and after is really too modern to work as a retro erotic look, with the possible exception of pop culture styles such as hippy or punk. Both originals and reproductions can be found on the Internet for all these periods, while it's not hard to get hold of a pattern and make them yourself, especially Victorian underwear, which would often have been homemade anyway.

Corsets

At the beginning of the 20th century the corset was an everyday item of feminine apparel, but declined from WWI onwards, vanishing almost completely by the 50s  only to re-emerge as fetish fashion wear in the 80s. Modern corsets are meant to be seen, at very least by your partner in private and often more openly. The one in the picture is a beautiful cream-coloured satin example from Axfords in Brighton, designed as underwear and not really suitable for the street. Other designs have cups, may be shorter or longer, and come in brilliant colours and many materials aside from silk and satin, including leather, rubber and even metal. Whatever the design, the aim is to enhance the curve of a woman's waist and so exaggerate her bust and hips, usually by pulling tight a system of laces at the back, providing a combination of sexual display and restriction with powerful fetish appeal.

Corsets are also useful for cross-dressing, as they create a feminine shape and it is also possible to find masculine corsets, which have quite a different shape. Whatever your taste, there are now plenty of corset makers to choose from, providing a wide range of products, many of which are reasonably priced, although the care and skill that goes into making a good quality corset does mean that you will get what you pay for.

Role Play

There's a lot of pleasure in fetish role play, recreating sexually charged scenarios or adding an erotic touch to any situation that takes your fancy. Maybe you just find certain outfits appealing and like to dress for sex, but many situations are ideal for power exchange, with you

 taking on roles that in real life would give one of you authority over the other and then thoroughly abusing it. I shouldn't really need to say this again, but there will always be a few people who get the wrong end of the stick, so let me stress that this is only play and bears no more relation to real abuse of power than paintball does to real war.

The perennial favourite is teacher and pupil. College uniform is easy to recreate and everybody is familiar with the way the game works, although a glance at the chapter on spanking may provide a few extra tips. Or you might like to explore the possibilities of other authority figures; bosses, police, priests, prison warders, maybe a gamekeeper with a freshly caught poacher. Some women find it exciting to pretend to be selling themselves, or being spied on, although if you're going to do this it really helps to make sure others can't get the wrong impression.

Some insist on an authentic look. Others prefer an erotic version.

If you prefer to let skill or chance decide who comes out on top, sports kit provides plenty of good looks; men in cricket whites and women in tennis gear being two old favourites, and you can always play the encounter out for real. Uniforms are so popular that they need to be dealt with separately, and then there are the possibilities offered by taking on an animal role, but those deserve their own chapter.

Because most role play scenarios are taken from real life it is usually easy to buy whatever you need, even if you want to dress as a bishop. Even if you prefer something unusual, the chances are it will be available online, while sex shops often have a range of role play outfits. One thing to bear in mind when buying is authenticity, especially if you're planning to dress up as a treat for your partner. Some people prefer a fully authentic look, so that a nurse's outfit, for example, would have to be the real thing, complete with a sensible skirt and upside-down watch. Others prefer an eroticised uniform, in which case the perfect sexy nurse comes in a rubber uniform with a skirt that barely covers her cheeks behind and a zip open to her belly button at the front.

Uniforms

There aren't many people who don't find a smart uniform appealing, or even a not-so-smart uniform, so not surprisingly it's often taken a step further. Not only do they look good, but uniforms are almost always associated with some sort of hierarchy, which makes them perfect for power exchange and role play. The obvious choice is the military, which for many people has become part of their everyday look, with combat trousers now as acceptable as jeans.

Although the military look is generally thought of as tough, suggesting a dominant image, it doesn't have to work that way. Just look at the illustration. In practice, it can work any way you want it to, while the different ranks

and services allow you to express who's in charge and fine tune your look or suit it to your body image.

If you want a really smart look, full dress uniform is worth exploring, with plenty of colour and striking lines. Naval whites work exceptionally well, as does British Army scarlet, but while black may be the smartest of all, most people feel that German WWII uniforms are in bad taste.

Police uniforms can be equally striking, but have the disadvantage that unless you stay firmly indoors, there's a chance of being arrested for impersonating an officer, and even if your uniform belongs to a different force from a different country questions are likely to be asked.

Army surplus stores are always good for uniforms, as are theatrical suppliers, while it's often surprising what you can pick up in charity shops. Braid can be made very easily, while accessories such as swagger sticks and spurs can be found with minimal effort. Swords are highly collectible and so quite easy to find, if expensive, but shouldn't be worn in public for obvious reasons. Similarly, carrying a gun, or anything that looks remotely like one, is a really, really bad idea.

Leather

Leather, and particularly black leather, is a fetish classic; sexy, edgy and rebellious, with an enduring popularity. Male or female, gay or straight, dominant or submissive and all points between, you can use leather garments to help express your sexuality, not just because of its versatility as a material, but by making use of the culture that has built up around it over the years. For some people, that may even be too blatant, but for others leather is not merely an accessory to a fetish lifestyle, but essential to their sexuality. The smell, the feel, the look, all combine to create a powerful need, so strong that it can become essential for arousal and orgasm – a fetish in the strictest sense of the word. Far more people, myself included, enjoy these same things without actually needing them, and if you haven't tried leather clothing I recommend at least giving it a go.

> With leather, the smell, the feel and the look can combine to create a powerful need, so strong that it can become essential for arousal and orgasm – a fetish in the strictest sense of the word.

There is plenty available, from mainstream gear such as boots and jackets, to trousers, waistcoats and more overtly sexual and specialist garments such as skin tight shorts and body harnesses. It's never particularly cheap and the quality can be very variable, while if you like anything other than black you may have difficulty finding the design you want. Fortunately, leather is quite easy to work. Anybody who can sew should be able to make leather gear with a little practice, and, while you will need specialist equipment, it's easy enough to find.

Alan, pictured at the London Fetish Fair, is wearing a leather jacket, kilt and boots, all handmade to his own

designs drawn from medieval originals. Leather is not cheap, and while imitations are available, they are never really satisfying. You also need different hides for different purposes, while something like a jacket takes skill and practice, but if leather is your thing it's definitely worth learning.

If you are thinking of exploring the world of fetish clubs, leather gear is often a sensible choice, especially for men. Clubs have dress-codes designed to keep out the idly curious, but will nearly always accept leather, which, in turn, can usually be worn in the street without causing comment. Better still, if you do want to go in high boots, skin tight shorts and nothing else, a long leather coat not only provides cover but added flair.

Rubber

Rubber is a wonderful material for erotic display, clinging to the body like a second skin, to display every contour in shiny black or brilliant colour. Genuine rubber fetishists are rare, but over the last 30 years it has grown to become

the material of choice for fetish fashion, with several firms vying to create the most fantastic garments for the underground and even edging into the mainstream market.

Because rubber is so tight, some might argue that it's very much a look for the beautiful people, but it also provides a lot of support and can not only reveal but enhance. It also holds its shape well when not tight to the body; making good pleats, frills etc, so that a skilled designer can always create a dramatic erotic image.

Perhaps the best designer of all is Robin of the House of Harlot, who has been around since the early 90s and offers an impressive range of highly imaginative rubber outfits. The rubber maid's outfit in the picture is one of their items, quite simple by their standards and just one of many, many designs. These are not cheap, but given the difficulty of working with rubber and the amount of work and imagination that goes into their outfits that is hardly surprising.

Rubber is also popular as a way of giving an extra dimension to other fetish looks, especially uniform, and it's possible to buy recreations of even elaborate military gear in rubber.

Unfortunately, rubber has its drawbacks. It's expensive, easy to damage and takes a great deal of care to maintain. It's also hard to work and very hard to work well, so much so that unless you have a great deal of time and skill it's impractical to make your own outfits, while anything glamorous will cost several hundred pounds. Rubber underwear is cheaper and more practical, but not the easiest look to carry off, while even if you buy it purely for fun in the privacy of your own bedroom it can become an expensive hobby.

> Rubber garments need looking after. They should be washed in cold, soapy water immediately after use and stored away from sunlight and too much heat.

Rubber garments need looking after and should be stored away from sunlight and extremes of temperature. Damaged rubber is not easy to repair. It tears easily and will eventually perish, so you need to be aware that your beautiful rubber outfit has a limited life.

When getting dressed in rubber, use plenty of talc and clean off the excess once you're done. Rubber is naturally glossy, but to get the super shiny look that gives it the edge you need to use a latex polish or silicone spray. Wearing rubber is hot, tight and sweaty, which is great if that's what gets you off, but otherwise is a nuisance, and you should always clean your outfit with warm, soapy water as soon as you take it off, or at the latest as soon as you've finished bonking each other senseless.

Accessories and Adornment

Every fetish look has it accessories, and sometimes it's the accessories that make the look. A smart suit and stern expression and you have a businessman. Put a cane in his hand and you have a male dom. The same goes for make-up, hairstyles, tattoos and other body adornments, all of which can be combined to enhance your look and allow you to create a fully developed fetish image, as shown

here by Jed Phoenix, who is also one of the most skilled and imaginative designers.

The choice is so wide that it's impossible to give more than rules of thumb, the most important of which is that things generally look better if they're co-ordinated. What does matter is where to go to get the things you might need. For any look drawn from the mainstream, the best bet is usually specialist shops, and it's cheaper and easier to kit yourself out as the perfect dominant riding mistress at a good equestrian centre than it is at a sex shop. Not only that, all but the best sex shops tend to go in for downmarket, even tacky, imitation gear yet still charge high prices. Better to go for the real thing.

If your look is drawn from another alternative culture there are plenty of options online and in any decent sized city. The more edgy street markets, such as London's Camden Lock, and particular districts, such as the Byres

Road area of Glasgow, are often good, especially for edgy but fashionable looks such as burlesque, while gear from shops aimed at subcultures such as Goth or Punk can often be adapted for fetish use. The same is true for jewellery, which can be highly imaginative, such as the pieces shown here from Birgit of Deadly Glamour.

If the look you want is pure fetish, you're going to  need a specialist or to learn to make things yourself. There are a few genuine fetish shops about, but you can find a much broader range of equipment, both for style and for price, from smaller outfits who operate online or run stalls as fetish markets such as the London Fetish Fair and London Alternative Market, or the Birmingham Bizarre Bazaar. These are exclusively for fetish gear, excellent places to shop and very relaxed and friendly. You can purchase just about anything you could possibly imagine, as long as it's kinky, or if your imagination goes further still you can order custom made equipment.

There's also a surprising amount of variety, with many small vendors attending only their local event, so that if you can't find what you want at one market you may well be able to at another. Much of what you'll see is handmade by the stallholders themselves, often to very high standards, or sourced from around the world. The vast majority of the people involved are genuine enthusiasts and will be able to give you all the advice you could possibly need on how to make the best of their products.

The picture shows Vicky and Cat of Freakclubwear in front of their stall at the London Fetish Fair. They sell clothes, jewellery and fetish equipment, making their outfit a one-stop shop for all but the most particular tastes.

Kinky Relationships

This is a practical guide, dealing with what to do rather than how to go about finding somebody to do it with, but I do want to say a few things about relationships that involve exotic sexual pleasures. The first, and most important point, is that they are really much the same as any other human relationship. Even with open relationships or polyamorous relationships, the only real difference is that the lines between being friends and being lovers becomes blurred. Otherwise, the most important thing is to find somebody who is compatible with you.

Being sexually adventurous or needing to express a particular fetish doesn't change the basic dynamic between men and women, it only makes it more complicated, while the idea of kinky people being up for anything and with anybody is a myth. Even on internet forums where communication is open and there are few taboos, such as the BDSM site Informed 'Consent, people react to each other much as they do in any other social group.

Generally speaking, for a woman to give her all, she needs to establish intimacy and trust first, which takes time, and this tends to remain true no matter what she likes to do once she feels ready. Crude or aggressive approaches tend to be off putting, just as they are in other circumstances. In one debate, about online chat, a woman wrote,*"It was the bra cup size request that always got me, so I used to reply "between 30aaa and 50ggg but by asking that question you're never going to find out."* To me, this sums up the most widespread feminine perspective, which is to want the person first. If the person is right, the act will follow.

Men, generally speaking, place greater stress on the physical, both in terms of the woman's body, and what she likes to do. That doesn't mean they don't want to be with somebody who can be a friend as well as a lover, or who has other things in common beyond the sexual, only that the initial attraction is more likely to be physical.

Neither of these attitudes is right or wrong. They are simply different, but male or female, to belittle your partner's perspective is to invite disaster. Successful relationships require mutual understanding, and this does not cease to be true because those involved have unusual tastes, just the opposite. After all, if you are a woman whose desire is to give herself over to a man's control so completely that you become, in effect, his slave, then it is hardly surprising that you will want him to be perfect. Likewise, if you are a man whose sexual satisfaction relies on beautiful female feet, then the first thing you will want to know about a potential partner is how she looks barefoot. Be tolerant, because if you want people to accept your foibles, life will be a lot easier if you're prepared to accept theirs.

Another common myth is that relationships which involve unconventional sex are somehow shallow or unfulfilling. In practice, there is no reason a less conventional relationship need be any less loving, just the opposite. Sharing exotic sexual practices and being completely open and honest about each other's sexuality can help to build an intimacy that goes far beyond the ordinary.

Tickled Pink

Sensation Play

The body has a great variety of senses, every one of which can be sexually stimulating just as long as the brain makes it so. To a scientist the old idea of the idea of the five senses – sight, sound, smell, taste and touch – is hopelessly out of date. The human eye alone contains five distinct types of photoreceptor; rods for light intensity, three types of cones to measure light of different wavelengths and thus allow us to see colour, and ganglion cells which relate to circadian rhythm. Without any one of these our concepts of erotic imagery would be very different, and it is only because they all work together that we can share concepts such as the perception of red as a sexual colour.

Just as the pain of a smack or the pressure of a tight rope can be delightful, horrible, or both at the same time, so can heat and cold, what we see, what we feel, and the input of every other sense.

The same is true of the other senses, both for direct stimulation and to trigger arousing memories. A sweet song and the scent of jasmine on the air may be wonderfully romantic, but how much more so if your first ever sexual experience was to the background of that same song and that same scent? Or it might be the taste of leather from a gag used when a partner used to spank you in your college hall. What matters is the association in your mind between the sensation and arousal. Just as the pain of a smack or the pressure of a tight rope can be delightful, horrible, or both at the same time, so can heat and cold, what we see, what we feel, and the input of every other sense. Internal senses, balance and proprioception, can also be arousing, such as when a blindfold is used to heighten feelings of apprehension and uncertainty, or with the sense of helplessness created by being in bondage and off balance. The art is to make best use of the sensation for arousal.

Strictly speaking, everything discussed in this book could come under the heading of sensation play, but from a practical point of view, some things are so popular that they deserve their own chapters while some only warrant a section. Also, some things are feasible, some less so, and no book could ever hope to list every possible combination of the different sensations, especially when they are often so personal. The best I can do is to offer a few ideas and some advice on how to put the more popular choices into practice.

> The art of sensation play is to make best use of a feeling for your arousal.

Most techniques concentrate on the skin, especially the erogenous zones, so it helps to understand how we register different sensations. Without going into too much scientific detail, we need to know that the skin contains numerous different types of nerve endings. Distinct nerve endings allow us to feel light touch, pressure, pain, cold and heat, all of which are separate sensations. Concentrations of these nerve endings vary across different parts of the body. The most sensitive areas of all are the hands, feet and face, but the genitals, anal area and nipples have a unique combination of nerve ending types, which is what makes those the primary erogenous zones. Other areas, such as the lips, chest, and the nape of the neck, have a similar but less concentrated pattern of sensitivity, which makes them secondary erogenous zones.

> Whatever sense you are dealing with, the way the brain interprets the signals you receive is crucial.

Whatever sense you are dealing with, the way the brain interprets the signals you receive is crucial, and can make an enormous difference. The simplest illustration of this is how we react to a touch from different people. A lover's touch is a delight, but exactly the same touch from somebody else can be repellent. There may be other signals involved, sight, perhaps smell or sound, but the main difference is in the mind.

> A lover's touch is a delight, but exactly the same touch from somebody else can be repellent.

It's possible to use this to play games. In the picture, Sophie is being fed chocolate, but she doesn't know it is chocolate, only that something is going to be put in her mouth. She'd been told the taste would be unpleasant, and thought it was until the sugar receptors on her tongue were giving a strong enough signal to convince her brain otherwise. You can easily imagine how this game can be extended to different sensations and to create different effects.

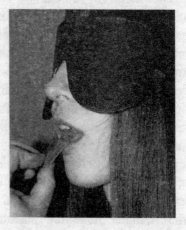

Which part of the body to use in sensation play depends on what you're doing, but it's not always best to go for the most sensitive areas, especially during foreplay or if you're in a situation where you're not comfortable with full intimacy. Very sensitive areas, particularly the genitals, are also easily injured. The bottom is often a good choice, strongly sexual but not especially sensitive, while a man's chest may not be as erotically potent as a woman's but provides similar feelings.

Communicate, test, and be ready to react to that safe word.

As with every other form of exotic sex, sensation play carries risks of which you need to be aware. Most of the time, this is common sense, but do think about what you want to do with a cool, clear head before getting down to it, and if you want to apply a sensation to somebody else, test it on yourself first. Another problem I've come across occasionally is allergic reactions, which can be to something as unexpected as nickel plating on bondage gear, so again, communicate, test, and be ready to react to that safe word.

Touch

Touch is basic to sex. Fingers stroked gently down the nape of your neck, hair nuzzled against your chest, your partner's lips against your own, or his or her tongue applied somewhere rather more intimate. It's all basic to sexual experience and not nearly kinky enough to fit in here. Even vibrators are now so accepted they can be shown on mainstream TV, but they can add a lot of extra fun to bondage or spanking sessions and there is one trick, which definitely deserves a mention. Remote controlled vibrators are available for as little as £20 and perfect for adding a twist to sex play with a mild D/s element, or better still, for use

Try outside, with the vibrator in place and never knowing when your partner is going to subject you to a barely controllable jolt of pleasure.

outside with the vibrator in place and never knowing when your partner is going to subject you to a barely controllable jolt of pleasure.

What also deserves a mention is the use of stroking and massage after an intense experience, particularly anything that's left you with hot, red skin. For instance, having a soothing cream rubbed into your bottom after a good spanking not only feels nice but can raise your feelings of intimacy or submission to a whole new level. Whatever you're doing, aftercare is always a good idea, even if it's just a cuddle, especially with very intense experiences, for which physical reassurance can be vital.

> Having a soothing cream rubbed into your bottom after a good spanking not only feels nice but can raise your feelings of intimacy or submission to a whole new level.

Tickling is little different to straightforward caresses, for most people, intimate but playful and not at all the stuff of scandal. Yet, for some, it's not just mild sex play but a fully formed fetish, even to the point of not being able to achieve arousal without it, whether it's tickling somebody, being tickled, or both. Tickling stimulates both the Meissner's corpuscles and free nerve endings in the skin, but there is also a strong psychological element to the reaction. Because of this, different people will react completely differently to the same action, say being tickled on the soles of the feet.

> For some people, tickling is a fully formed fetish.

Those few who are not ticklish at all may be indifferent, and others will find it merely irritating, but for the right person, with the right partner, it can be intensely erotic.

This is not a simple reaction. For some it may be the

physical sensation and the resultant release of endorphins that turns them on, for others it may be being rendered helpless, so that tickling becomes a gesture of dominance and even playful cruelty.

If you're having your nipples, genitals or anal area tickled, the reaction is different, because as you grow aroused your erogenous zones grow less ticklish. The skin structure here is different, not as sensitive as the most ticklish areas of all, but with an arrangement of nerve endings, especially corpuscles, which send sexual signals to the brain. Because the signals change and your ticklishness fades, tickle play is often best aimed at other parts of the body, especially the soles of the feet and palms of the hands, under the arms and behind the knees and elbows, while more vigorous tickling works best on the flanks and belly.

> As you grow aroused, your erogenous zones grow less ticklish.

Your fingers are really all you need for tickling, and your hair can also be good for more sensitive areas, so, for once, this is something you can do without specialist equipment. Just about anything with a fine point, or preferably lots of fine points, will work for tickling – leaves, fur, the tip of a pen, a paintbrush – but the classic tickling implement has to be a feather.

Feathers work best on the most sensitive areas of the skin, especially the nipples and the tuck of the bottom cheeks,

> Feathers work best on the most sensitive areas of the skin, especially the nipples and the tuck of the bottom cheeks.

individually, or for a less subtle effect, using a feather duster. The flight feathers of birds such as pigeons and crows are the easiest to get hold of, but they don't work particularly well. Display feathers from a peacock's tail are far better, and more stylish, but the best of all has to be ostrich, perhaps employed as illustrated, with a couple of bushy feathers applied to the tuck of your partner's bottom, which we found to be highly effective, reducing

Sarah to such helpless giggling that she could barely keep still for the photo.

If you like something a little more vigorous, stiff brushes are a good way to stimulate the skin and work well as a D/s game. Try it in a Dickensian style, with one of you as the matron or a prison guard and the other stripped for a vigorous scrubbing in the bath, perhaps with a little spanking thrown in to produce a fresh, hot glow that makes a great prelude to wet sex. Clawed gloves and other accessories designed to stimulate the skin have a similar effect, but stronger sensations need to be dealt with separately.

Pain

For most people it's instinctive to recoil in horror at the thought of associating pain with sex, but who hasn't enjoyed love bites or scratching in the heat of passion?

> Who hasn't enjoyed love bites or scratching in the heat of passion?

Pain stimulates the release of endorphins into the body, which can be highly erotic if the pain is relatively mild and, crucially, given in the right context. Nevertheless, you do need to take care, especially as those same endorphins that bring you so much pleasure can make you unaware of damage.

> Because of this risk, with any form of play that involves pain it is the responsibility of the top to ensure that nothing goes wrong.

Because of this risk, with any form of play that involves pain it is the responsibility of the top to ensure that nothing goes wrong. The more intense the experience, the more important this is, so whatever you want to do, be sure to negotiate in advance, test any techniques or equipment you want to use on yourself and pay close attention to your partner's reactions.

The simplest forms of pain play are scratching, biting and pinching. Scratching and biting in particular are often done in the heat of the moment, but all three can also be more deliberate and used not only as mutual stimulation but to assert dominance. Pinching especially has overtones of sexual dominance, especially to the bottom or nipples, hence the justified outrage of anybody who's had their bottom pinched by an unwelcome hand.

> Any injury beyond the trifling and transient sustained for the sake of sexual pleasure could be treated as assault regardless of consent.

Often, the most popular use of pain as sex play comes from giving somebody a smacked bottom, so much so in fact that spanking deserves its own chapter. Other practices fall firmly under the title of edge play, and you should always bear in mind that any injury beyond the trifling and transient sustained for the sake of sexual pleasure could be treated as assault, regardless of consent. A good general rule is never to do anything that breaks the skin, but the most important thing is to be aware of what you're doing and the risks involved.

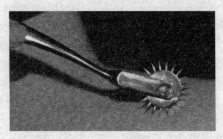

If you do find pain or the idea of pain stimulating, a good intro-duction to pain play is the Wartenburg Pin Wheel, which is ideal for gauging your own tolerance or that of your partner before trying anything more severe. The example in the picture was bought at the London Alternative Market for £12 from Affordable Leather Products and is made of surgical steel. In the picture, you can see how it presses down onto the flesh, which produces a sharp, prickling sensation. They work best on the secondary erogenous zones, particularly the bottom and chest and are great for slow foreplay. Used firmly, they can puncture the skin, so it's important to sterilise your equipment before and after play. I would count anything designed to draw blood, such as needles, or with an exceptionally potent social and psychological significance, such as knives, as edge play and so beyond the scope of this book. If you do want to experiment,

Always sterilise your equipment before and after play. This is doubly important if the same piece of equipment is to be used on more than one person and when playing with anybody other than a regular partner.

62

learn as much as you can first. There is plenty of advice available.

Another popular form of pain play is to use substances that irritate the skin. As always, this requires a bit of common sense. Avoid the eyes and other very sensitive areas, test everything on yourself before making it a part of sex play and be ready to stop and take appropriate action if things go wrong. A wide range of substances can be used to make your skin feel hot and sensitive, or sting, or prickle: preparations such as Ralgex or Tiger Balm, plants like ginger and chilli, even some brands of toothpaste. Each substance has its own properties, but the idea is to make the skin sensitive and boost endorphin production. Whatever you choose, try it on the skin of your back or bottom first and work gradually up to the thighs, chest and nipples. Only if you're comfortable with the resulting sensations should you consider applying anything to your genitals, and even then, take it slowly.

> The best pain play mixes the physical sensation with an emotional element.

The best of this sort of play mixes the physical sensation with an emotional element. A good example is using ginger root for what's called figging. The juice from ginger root is mildly stimulating to ordinary skin but produces a strong burning sensation on the nipples or genitals. Figging involves carving a piece of ginger root into the shape of a small plug, which fits into your bottom, mixing the intimacy and possibly embarrassment of anal penetration with the burn of the ginger juice. Usually this is part of a complicated and deliberately cruel punishment ritual, with the piece of ginger, or fig, inserted before you're given six of the best while in a position that leaves your cheeks open and the base of the fig showing.

The burning sensation is supposed to stop you clenching your bottom cheeks as well, although this doesn't necessarily work.

Spiky plants can always be put to good use, although some are better than others. Gorse prickles are too fine and can easily break off in your skin, causing irritation long after you want it to stop. Thorn bushes, brambles and roses are too vicious for most tastes, with large, hard thorns that easily break the skin. Holly is just about right, pleasantly prickly on the skin, while the large, irregular leaves are perfect for stuffing down your underwear during a country walk, or simply applying direct, as in the picture.

Nettling goes a step further and is another game also frequently linked to erotic punishment rather than simply used as stimulation. Stinging nettle leaves are coated with tiny hairs that puncture the skin to inject a cocktail of chemicals – methanoic acid, histamine, acetylcholine and serotonin – which combine to produce a stinging, burning sensation and to cause localised inflammation of the flesh, commonly known as nettle rash. The Common Stinging Nettle, *Urtica dioica*, can be found throughout the UK and in most other parts of the world, but there are other species as well, some of which cause a much stronger reaction. Nettles are at their most potent when freshly grown in the spring and less when dying down in the autumn.

Being nettled is a very intense experience indeed, but it is also deceptive. When the nettles first touch you feel only a mild tickling, but this quickly builds up to a sharp, stinging sensation, then comes the heat and a powerful throbbing, which can combine to create an extraordinarily powerful and erotic effect, although you must have the right mindset for this to work or it will simply be painful and unpleasant.

Never put nettles anywhere near your face, and use them sparingly, either with a single nettle drawn gently over the skin or with a 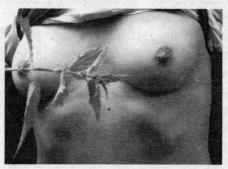 small bunch applied to a single area of the body, perhaps just the bottom or chest. Nettle spines are more likely to penetrate the skin when touched gently than hard, so while a nettle whipping may be emotionally strong, tickling is more effective. A good scenario would be to have your partner tied with her hands behind a tree, bare chested while you use a single, freshly picked nettle, teasing for a while before touching it to her skin and slowly building up, perhaps before bringing her to climax with her entire chest hot and swollen.

Nettle spines can break off in the skin and cause problems, although this is rare. There is also a risk of an allergic reaction, so never do it unless you know for certain that you don't react badly to histamine or any of the other active ingredients. In fact, I'd advise against it unless you've been stung plenty of times and know you can cope easily. Even then, there is a major drawback, because the stinging, throbbing sensation lasts for several hours, so you're likely to end up lying on your front feeling sorry for yourself at five o'clock in the morning while your partner is snoring happily beside you.

Pressure and Tension

Pressure and tension might not seem very sexy sensations, but they play a crucial part in vanilla sex and in kink too. The feeling of being full when penetrated is all to do with pressure and stretch receptors in the skin and muscles, and for women in particular, that is a major part of sexual pleasure. That's not to say the boys can't play too, and penetration can be so much more than straight, vanilla sex.

If you like things inside you, boy or girl, anal or vaginal, there's one basic, never to be ignored rule: if you are going to stretch an orifice beyond its normal capacity, take it slowly and use plenty of lubricant. It's also important to use the right lubricant, preferably something water based and purpose made. Never be rough, especially with anal play, which should not be painful. If it is,

> If you are going to stretch an orifice beyond its normal capacity, take it slowly and use plenty of lubricant.

stop. If there is internal damage you probably won't feel it, so if there is any bleeding after anal sex seek medical attention immediately.

The anal area is well supplied with sensory receptors much like those in the genitals and linked to the same major nerve, so it is a primary erogenous zone, while the interior of the rectum is adjacent to the rear of the genitals, particularly the prostrate gland in men. So there's plenty of fun to be had without considering the taboo of anal play, which adds a whole new dimension. Even exposure can be an intense thrill, combining vulnerability and humiliation, but that's so closely linked to punishment that it belongs in the section on spanking.

Penetration with small objects can work in the same way, as a humiliation in its own right, or so that you remain aware that you are being held open for something bigger.

Any smooth, firm object of the right dimensions will serve, but never use anything which might break or form a vacuum trap and get stuck. The commonest problem of this type is when a woman uses a bottle to penetrate herself, as the contractions of the vaginal muscles during orgasm can draw air from the bottle and create a vacuum too hard to break without risking damage. If this does happen to you, go straight to A&E. Never mind the embarrassment.

It's much better to use purpose made dildos or plugs, which come in a wide variety of sizes, shapes and textures. Some vibrate, some are inflatable, some are designed to help with practices too kinky even for this book. Some are huge, but I would advise very strongly against doing anything that stretches your muscles beyond their normal capacity, particularly for anal play as not only is there a risk of damage, but if you do it too often, you may become incontinent.

The human hand is just about at the limit of what is sensible for vaginal play, although if you've had children you can probably cope without difficulty. This is called fisting and is particularly popular with lesbian couples. It's also popular with a lot of men, but will cause problems if you overdo it. For a woman to accept a fist in her vagina she needs to be both relaxed and aroused, so fisting is best done after plenty of foreplay as well as with plenty of

> Fisting can produce sensations of fullness, satisfaction, vulnerability and more.

lubricant. The knack is to close your fingers together at the tips, making your hand into a long cone which can be worked gradually inside. Your hand should be rotated gently as it goes in, particularly to get your knuckles past the pubic bone. Once you're in, your fingers can form a fist, sometimes with the thumb between index and middle fingers, which you can twist or draw slowly back and forth, perhaps while you bring her to orgasm. Fisting can produce sensations of fullness, satisfaction, vulnerability and more, because as always the pleasure can be as much about what's going on in your head as your body. Mind your fingernails!

Pressure play can also work on other parts of the body. Many people enjoy being sat on, for the physical intimacy of the act, for the sense of being under their partner's control and for the physical pressure of their weight on your body.

The favourite practice of this type is for a woman to sit on a man's face, and for

> Be careful, because when smothered between a pair of ample cheeks, he may be in heaven but he probably can't breathe very easily, if at all.

many men, the fuller the bottom the better. Be careful though, because when smothered between a pair of ample cheeks, he may be in heaven but he probably can't breathe very easily, if at all. You also need to keep most of your weight on your knees, and to leave his hands free so that he can signal if there's a problem.

Most other forms of pressure play relate closely to pain, especially those which pinch the flesh. Clothes pegs work well for this, especially wooden ones, producing a sharp nipping sensation that quickly becomes dulled only to be followed by a much stronger ache when the peg is removed and the blood flows back into the pinched flesh. If you like something a little more elegant, it is possible to buy purpose made clamps, for general use, for nipples and for genitals. These come in a wide variety of designs and are often linked by chains or supplied with weights which can be used to make the sensation still more intense.

The picture shows a set of nipple clamps from Affordable Leather Products. They have rubber tipped jaws so that there's no risk of breaking the skin and are joined by a system of steel chains and a ring which add their own weight to the effect or can be used to make further attachments. This set cost £25, basic clamps can be as little as £10, but it's possible to buy full sets including small weights designed to hang from your  nipples, complicated devices to pull on them, or with a tray attached to allow you to serve food nibbles and drinks with your clamped breasts on show. If you can imagine it, somebody probably makes it.

Pressure can also be an important element of bondage, but that is dealt with separately.

Cold

The skin contains specialised receptors for cold, with a peak sensitivity of around $-40^\circ C$, but for sex play you should stick to temperatures around $0^\circ C$ or there is a risk of frostbite. Ice is perfect for cold play, not only because of its melting point, but because water takes up heat only very slowly, so that while most cold objects will warm up too fast for extended sex play a piece of ice will melt only gradually. Frozen gases – carbon dioxide, oxygen, nitrogen or anything else – are far too cold for safe play.

When playing with ice, use relatively small pieces, such as cubes from an ordinary freezer tray. Roll these in your hand before touching them to your partner's body, both to

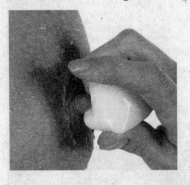
melt away any sharp edges and to make sure the surface of the ice isn't so cold it will stick to the skin.

Nipples just cry out to be iced, very sensitive and very sexual. Just a touch is often enough to get full erection. The picture shows a piece of freezer ice, smoothed in a warm hand and then applied to Ivy's nipple. Apparently it was very cold indeed, and her response was as delightful as the more obvious reaction.

Ice cream is great for sexy games on a summer's day.

Ice can also be used to good effect on hot skin, and generally works well as a counterpoint to heat play. Best of all are ice balls, which you might like to apply to your partner's bottom, perhaps after a spanking, before popping them into vagina or anus, and, of course, you don't have to worry about getting them out afterwards.

Frozen food can work as well as ice, and better if you like things a little messy. Ice cream is great for sexy games on a summer's day, and being made to go out in a skirt with a packet of frozen peas down your knickers makes an excellent punishment. Snow can also be a lot of fun, both for D/s games such as making your partner strip and go out in it, or if your relationship is more equal, fighting to get snowballs down each other's clothes.

Heat

Heat stimulates specific receptors as well as the free nerve endings, producing a unique sensation and leaving the skin highly sensitive. The heat receptors in human skin give the strongest response at around 40°C, above which the sense of warmth begins to die down and is replaced with a pain reaction from the free nerve endings. Anything at a temperature of 50°C or more is liable to cause burns, so the safe and practical range of temperature for heat play is

With any form of heat play you should put safety very firmly first.

71

between 35 and 50°C, although even within this range you should avoid prolonged exposure.

Using naked flame is out of the question for sex play, as while fire-eaters and other performers can play with fire safely enough, this requires perfect control and does not mix well with arousal. Hot substances are more practical but with any form of heat play you should put safety very firmly first. Think out what you are going to do in advance, prepare and test your equipment and make sure you have plenty of water close to hand. If you do burn your skin run the affected area under cold water for at least a minute in order to draw the energy out of your flesh.

With wax, it is important to use the right sort. Different types of wax burn at different temperatures.

The most popular sort of heat play is to use wax on skin, which can be intensely erotic and is relatively safe, but it is important to gain a full understanding of what you are doing before you try it. It is important to use the right wax, because different types of wax burn at different temperatures.

Cheaper candles, usually made of soft paraffin wax, are best for wax play as they burn at 50-60°C, meaning the wax will cool into the safe range before it touches the skin. This will produce a sharp, stinging sensation as well as warmth but will not damage your skin.

For a first wax play experience, I'd recommend the back, which makes a broad canvas.

Coloured and scented candles will produce hotter wax, while beeswax and other expensive waxes have higher melting points and are likely to cause burns, so should be avoided. Wax cools rapidly as a drop falls through the air, so the effect will be milder the further the candle is held away from the skin. It should go without saying that you should only play with wax when sober, *never* apply wax to the genitals or face, and *always* test a few drops on your own skin first before using it on your partner. It's best to play nude to avoid ruining any clothing and where there's no risk of setting light to anything. A tiled floor is ideal and also easy to clean afterwards.

For a first wax play experience, I'd recommend the back, which makes a broad canvas. Apply the first few drips from as high as you can hold the candle

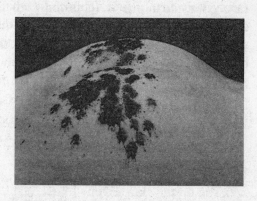

and lower it very slowly, aiming each drop so that it falls on fresh skin. You'll soon find what works for both of you and can move on to more erotic play.

The bottom cheeks are ideal for wax play, unless very hairy. When we waxed Sophie's bottom, as shown in the picture, we used a purple paraffin wax candle held no less than two feet above her skin, which produced a delightful sensation and left no marks at all.

With a very cool wax and a little practice it's possible to build a woman a wax bra. Building up a layer of wax produces a deeper, more lasting heat, and wax play is a slow game, so making the wax bra makes for gradually rising levels of

> Making a wax bra makes for gradually rising levels of excitement spread over as much as half-an-hour – perfect kinky foreplay.

excitement spread over as much as half-an-hour – perfect kinky foreplay.

Being tied up or blindfolded makes the experience even more intense, but you should be very sure that you are able to release your partner within a few seconds if necessary. Leather cuffs are probably better than rope for this purpose, and easier to clean if you get wax on them. One good technique is to fasten your partner's wrists to the bathroom sink, especially if you have a tiled floor, which means they're helpless but in the safest possible environment.

Peeling the wax off can also be fun, but can be a problem with hairy skin. A little massage oil rubbed in before you start to play makes removing the wax easier and adds to the fun, but can make droplets of wax run on the skin. Even after the wax has been removed, the skin stays exceptionally sensitive for quite a while, enhancing anything from the gentlest caress to a vigorous spanking.

> Even after the wax has been removed, the skin stays exceptionally sensitive for quite a while, enhancing anything from the gentlest caress to a vigorous spanking.

Cleaning up afterwards can be a nuisance and wax is very hard to get out of carpets and clothes, another good reason for using a tiled floor or a non-flammable splash mat. If you can, go out in the garden. On the plus side, you can leave candles lying about without risking a raised eyebrow from even the most prudish of visitors, while a suitably shaped candle does have other uses, of course...

Electroplay

Many people regard playing with electricity as too

dangerous to be considered safe, and I would advise very strongly against it unless you know exactly what you are doing. Yet the equipment is available and electroplay can be exquisite, so I feel it's better to provide some advice than simply to ignore the subject. Always put safety first, learn the rules and stick to them, without deviation.

Use only purpose built equipment designed specifically for use on the human body and in good working order.

Never, *under any circumstances*, play with mains electricity supply, or any other high power source. It is the current, measured in amps, that is dangerous, not the voltage. As little as 0.05 of an amp can be lethal, while many household appliances take 3 amps. Even 0.01 of an amp can be dangerous. If you don't understand these terms, don't play.

Always play on an insulated surface and make sure there is no risk of contact with any conductor, especially metal or water. Touching a conductor will make your body part of the circuit and result in electrocution.

Do not play if anyone involved has implanted medical devices, heart problems, nervous conditions such as epilepsy, or is on any medication that might place strain on the heart.

Do not play in situations where you might be jogged, causing the current to take an unexpected path. Electroplay is not suitable for clubs or any crowded environment.

When playing, avoid the head and neck, broken or grazed skin and moist areas.

If you follow the above advice scrupulously you will be able to play safely. The most popular device for electroplay is the violet wand. This converts mains electricity to a low current, high voltage output transmitted through a glass electrode filled with gas. When the device is on, the gas glows, usually violet, hence the name, but also other colours. The voltage can usually be controlled and varies from 10,000 to 50,000 V. The frequency is also high at around 200kHz (200,000 cycles per second), which is too high to cause muscle contractions.

The violet wand was originally invented in the late 19th century as an electrotherapy device and reached the height of its popularity in the 1920s and 30s. Although later examples exist, many of those you will come across are antiques and therefore need to be fully overhauled by people who know exactly what they're doing before use. The example in the picture was manufactured in Germany

around 1930 and comes from violet wand specialists,

Nick and Morphia. All of their stock is carefully tested and renovated as necessary before being put on sale.

As you can see, a wide variety of electrodes are available, each of which has a subtly different effect. The wand itself is turned on and alive with a brilliant orange glow, although in the picture this appears as if the electrode is filled with cloudy fluid. This is a high quality, versatile set and costs £600, while a simple set might be £200. Electroplay does not come cheap, but enthusiasts think it well worth the cost.

> On a low setting, the wand produces no more than a gentle tickling sensation, pleasant and stimulating but largely physical except on very sensitive areas.

It's certainly arousing. On a low setting, the wand produces no more than a gentle tickling sensation, pleasant and stimulating but largely physical except on very sensitive areas. As the voltage is increased the wand begins to stimulate the free nerve endings and heat receptors, producing a warm, prickling sensation. Higher still and it is sufficiently painful to be used as a psychological toy, to tease or threaten, while I find that even at a moderate level my endorphins kicked in after just a couple of minutes of play.

Technique can make all the difference, and while a wand is best tested by drawing the tip over the skin of your arm, the back and legs react particularly well, while a single precise touch can bring a nipple to aching erection. This works through clothing as well as on the bare skin. In general, the higher the voltage the more rapidly the wand should be moved over the skin, but by using different

> A single precise touch of a violet wand can bring a nipple to aching erection.

77

electrodes at different voltages and in different ways you can create a wide range of sensations and what works best for one individual may not be ideal for another. Personally, I found having the wand at high power and drawn rapidly across my skin best, as this produces a sharp, cutting sensation, painful enough to be exciting and to work as a gesture of dominance but not unendurable. When tied up, the psychological effect is stronger still.

Another technique is what is known as secondary contact, when you hold the wand in your hand, which makes your body live, with the electricity flowing over the surface of your skin. Any touch to your body will then tingle, whether it's from your partner's fingers or any conductive object. This makes for an intensely erotic experience, as every slightest caress is literally charged with electricity.

> Every tiny caress is charged with electricity.

There are other forms of electroplay. Transcutaneous Electrical Nerve Stimulator (TENS) machines deliver small electrical impulses to the body via electrodes placed on the skin, thus stimulating endorphin production. These are designed for medical use, or as pain relief, but can be used safely for erotic purposes if you know exactly what you're doing. E-Stim Systems are more advanced, with purpose built electrical stimulation devices designed specifically for sex play, including internal probes, remote control devices and more. These are generally considered to be edge play and it is essential that you take expert advice and learn to play safely before you begin.

Sex & Humiliation

Erotic humiliation is not easy to explain. If you don't appreciate it, you will never be able to understand it, but if you do, it makes perfect sense. It's like a spark in the mind, linking arousal to acts which would normally be embarrassing, even appalling. This may be a psychological defence mechanism, allowing you to turn an unpleasant experience around by making it pleasurable, but that doesn't really explain people's yearning to have such things happen to them when they could easily be avoided. So great is this apparent contradiction that many people find it difficult to cope with, but the answer lies in accepting yourself as you are, which can give sexual pleasure a whole new dimension. Take spanking as an example. Some people like being spanked but don't find it humiliating at all, while for others humiliation is what makes spanking erotic. That opens up all sorts of intriguing possibilities, which I'll come back to later.

From the dominant viewpoint, taking pleasure in other people's embarrassment or humiliation presumably derives from the desire to do better than your competitors, while blushing, laughing and other symptoms of embarrassment are also associated with sexual arousal. For those with a good sense of empathy, particularly if they enjoy erotic humiliation themselves, there is also the pleasure of knowing how your partner feels, which tempts you to act to make those feelings stronger.

What you must take in, if you are going to play with somebody who enjoys erotic humiliation but you don't understand it yourself, is that circumstances are everything. In the wrong place, at the wrong time, with the wrong person, an act will be completely unacceptable, just as it would be for anyone else, but in the right place, at the right time, with the right people, that same act will be ecstasy. Perhaps the best example is male on male fellatio, which is a popular piece of erotic humiliation for submissive men. The glib explanation of this is that the man has suppressed homosexual tendencies and is really only trying to find an excuse to express them, but anybody who understands erotic humiliation will realise that this is nonsense. Sucking a cock is obviously a sexual act, and can easily be perceived as a submissive act, but for a straight, submissive man to have his dominant girlfriend make him suck another man is an act of submission to her, in which the other man is no more than a bit player. The boyfriend is not enjoying the act of sucking the other man's cock, he is enjoying the erotic humiliation of sucking another man's cock, and what makes that erotic humiliation so powerful is that he's *not* gay. If he was gay, or bisexual, the same scene would simply be sex play. Having said all that, no doubt there are plenty of men who use erotic submission as an excuse to indulge gay male desires, both knowingly and subconsciously.

If you enjoy exotic sex, you're sure to encounter people who enjoy erotic humiliation, probably sooner rather than later, so it's important to appreciate how it works even if you don't understand it yourself. This is particularly important for the remaining chapters of the book as, for many of the sections, erotic humiliation is important to taking pleasure in the acts described, and in some cases essential. When erotic humiliation is involved, aftercare is more important than ever, so always be ready with a cuddle.

Bound and Gagged

Restraint & the Art of Bondage

Would you like to be helpless in your lover's arms, unable to resist either physically or mentally? Or would you like to have them as your plaything, body tight in restraint and available to you in every way?

To a great many people the answer to one of these questions will be a resounding yes, often to both. As a sexual fantasy, restraint comes second in popularity only to having conventional sex with an attractive partner, while many people have tried at least light bondage and there is less social stigma attached to it than to other kinks. At the other end of the scale, bondage can be one of the most elaborate and intense sexual practices of all, requiring extraordinary expertise and capable of reaching the level of an art form.

> Trust in your partner is never more important than during a bondage session. Never allow anybody to render you helpless unless you are 100% certain they will respect your limits.

The background to sexual restraint goes deep into our past, probably from long before we were sentient, and has now become part of out cultural heritage – often a dark, sinister part, but a part nonetheless, and as always my philosophy is to take that darkness and turn it into pleasure.

The commonest reason for enjoying restraint is the sense of helplessness it brings, often for its own sake, but sometimes because if you are helpless then what happens to you is no longer your responsibility. The two feelings are not mutually exclusive, but they are very different. Helplessness for its own sake can provoke a multitude of strong feelings; surrender, apprehension, shame, defiance, panic and more, all of which are sexual in the context of erotic bondage. For those who also like to give up their responsibility, they can then enjoy all these emotions, and whatever is done to them while tied up, without the guilt that has come to be associated with sex in our culture. Of course, you might still feel guilty about letting yourself be put in bondage, but it seems to me deliciously ironic that the idea of sex as somehow wrong, shameful or sinful is one of the things that makes being restrained so appealing.

It seems to me deliciously ironic that the idea of sex as somehow wrong, shameful or sinful is one of the things that makes being restrained so appealing.

The actual feeling of being restrained can also be pleasurable, especially when the restraints are applied so that they provide sexual stimulation. If done cleverly, it is possible to render your partner incapable of moving without stimulating themselves, an example of predicament bondage, which we'll come to later. Bondage can also be purely practical, when somebody is held captive, immobilised as a punishment or for punishment, or perhaps put in a position that causes feelings of exposure or erotic humiliation. This is often part of role-play, for instance when used to enhance prison, hospital or dungeon fantasies.

Some people also find that being in bondage enhances their feelings of sexual submission, although the opposite is true for those who feel that complete submission is only possible if they have complete freedom of choice, including movement. This can be extraordinarily intense, especially in tight bondage, to the point at which your mind seems to move to another place, an exquisite experience, but one that can also be frightening, so take care.

> Many enthusiasts have an interest in the aesthetics of bondage.

Bondage can also serve as an affirmation of trust between partners, as an element of other erotic games, to delay orgasm or draw out an experience, to restrict voyeurs during an erotic display, as a soothing experience and no doubt for many other things. As always with human sexuality, there is astonishing variety.

Putting somebody into bondage can also provide pleasure in a variety of ways, which can be more or less sexual. Control, power and access to a partner's body are the obvious benefits, while many enthusiasts also have an interest in the aesthetics of bondage, focussed both on the beauty of their partner's restrained body and the patterns of rope or systems of straps, even on complexity for its own sake. That's what makes bondage the most technical of kinks, with a multitude of variations on the theme and a jargon all its own.

It also requires a great deal of care and attention on the part of the top. Much of this is common sense, but it still bears repeating. First and foremost, if your partner is helpless, his or her welfare becomes your responsibility. Listen,, judge the responses of the body and always respect a safe word. Stay sober and clear-headed. Never, under any circumstances whatsoever,

> If your partner is helpless, his or her welfare becomes your responsibility.

restrict somebody's breathing or place anything around the neck that might lead to choking. Avoid applying

> Never, under any circumstances whatsoever, restrict somebody's breathing.

pressure to parts of the body where the veins and nerves run close under the skin, or there will be a risk of cutting off circulation. If you are using rope, choose something soft and flexible, not too thin, and don't tie it too tight. It should always be possible to slide a finger between rope and flesh. Work slowly and smoothly to avoid rope burn, using knots that prevent slipping or tightening.

When your partner is tied up, be careful to ensure that he or she cannot fall over, which is the commonest bondage accident. The second commonest is to have something break because there is too much weight on it, so never have more than a little of your partner's body weight supported by ordinary restraints. If you do want to raise somebody off the ground, make very sure that the system is strong enough. This cage, in the Barnet Bastille, is welded steel and held up on a pulley designed to lift truck engines, allowing even the heaviest people to be raised safely. It has also been thoroughly tested, which you should always do, using several times

the weight it will actually have to support. It only takes one weak link for a whole system to fail.

Never leave anyone alone when he or she is unable to escape, nor for too long. Always agree a safe word before you start and be ready to act on it immediately, even if it means damaging your equipment.

For most people, the purpose of bondage will be for

Bondage Safety Rules

Take care of your partner, let her know you are aware of her feelings and always be ready to release her and to comfort her if necessary. You are in control, so put her needs first, and remember:

Never restrict her airways.
Never risk cutting off her circulation.
Never keep her in bondage for over an hour.
Never leave her on her own while in bondage.
Never have her full weight supported by restraints.
Never risk her falling when she is unable to protect herself.

restraint in order to provide sexual access, in which case cuffs or simple ties are all you will need. Safety is still important, but it becomes more so with increasingly elaborate bondage, especially advanced rope bondage. I've set out the basics here, along with illustrative examples, but anybody wishing to explore the subject fully should purchase a specialist book. In any case, always start slowly, learn the basics before you try anything too elaborate and make sure you get plenty of practice.

Restriction

Bondage can be used to restrict rather than restrain. In the world of fashion, almost exclusively female fashion, the wearer's vulnerability is often accentuated by minor restraints. Many examples of this exist from history, such as the elaborate Victorian combinations of corsetry and skirt support which not only emphasised a woman's figure but made it difficult for her to do anything without assistance. Nowadays, it is more common to use imagery associated with full bondage, such as collars or boots fitted with loops or even D-rings.

High heels are a common and mainstream form of restriction.

Fetishists take these things further, deliberately designing clothing to restrict movement. The best known example must be high heels, which are designed to enhance your appearance and to restrict your movement, so very fetishistic despite being mainstream other than in their most exaggerated form. Another good example is the hobble skirt, which evolved from a tight, knee length skirt which obliged the wearer to take small, neat steps. Now, it is perfectly acceptable as office wear, to very tight, ankle length garments of leather or rubber that not only make it almost impossible to walk but reveal every contour of the wearer's figure. It may seem curious that this imagery is often associated with dominant women, but that

A rubber hobble skirt can restrict movement to tiny, precise steps.

seems to have more to do with erotic display than restriction, except in that being restricted can also imply high status because it shows that you don't do manual work. History is full of examples, such as the exaggeratedly long fingernails once cultivated by the Chinese aristocracy.

Restriction can be taken a step further with the use of devices such as spreaders, rigid bars with a cuff at either end which fix between your wrists, or your ankles in such a way that you are unable to close your legs, rendering you accessible as well as vulnerable. Likewise, having your hands tied or fixed apart makes it impossible to protect yourself although you are still able to walk.

In the picture, Sophie has a 15 inch spreader bar fixed between her ankles, enhancing her vulnerability as she dances. If you're going to do this, bear in mind that you really are more vulnerable, that you need to move carefully and should keep a good grip on the pole.

The "monoglove" takes this idea further still. It is a sheaf of material encasing your arms, which are usually held together behind your back. More elaborate still is the maid's bondage tray, where a tray is fixed just below chest height, with chains leading to a collar and wrist cuffs, maybe also ankles, even nipples, allowing the maid to serve drinks but do little else.

The bondage tray is a simple example of a specialist harness, bondage gear designed to restrict the wearer to specific functions. This can be overtly sexual, such as combined hip and head harness designed to keep the wearer in position to give oral sex but otherwise helpless, but most often goes with elaborate erotic games such as pony play, for which the harness is designed to mimic a horse harness but adapted for the human form. We'll come back to that.

Gags

A gag is usually intended to stop the wearer from speaking, but for erotic bondage is as often intended to make speaking difficult rather than impossible, or it can be purely symbolic. If you are going to gag somebody you do need to be careful. Always make sure the wearer can breathe freely, and it is absolutely essential that whatever is in the mouth cannot be swallowed. Never leave people alone if they're unable to remove a gag of

their own accord. The mouth is

A gag can be functional, or it can be purely symbolic.

one of the most delicate and sensitive parts of the body, so be exceptionally careful if a gag has metal parts or anything which might risk abrasion or damage to teeth.

The simplest type of gag is the cloth gag, for which a length of cloth is pulled tight across the mouth and tied off behind the head. It's crude, reasonably effective and can be done quickly, all of which makes it good for domestic play. Bands of broad tape pulled over the mouth and around the head are more effective but less suitable for sex play because tape can cause irritation to the delicate skin around the mouth and can even leave blemishes unless removed with care. Far more popular than either of the above is the ball gag, which is most often associated with bondage. This is a plastic ball, often with holes in it to make breathing easier, held in the mouth with straps and fastened off behind the head. A bar gag is similar, but with a plastic rod that fits between the

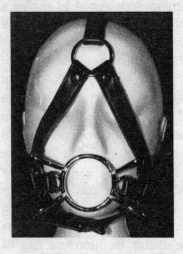

wearer's teeth like a horse's bit, and there is also the ring gag, in which the ball is replaced by a plastic ring so that the wearer's mouth stays open. The picture shows a variation of this, a spider gag, which has a central ring and four curved prongs in stainless steel with a head harness to hold it in place. It cost £30 from Trainer Bryan's stall at the London Alternative Market.

With some versions of the ball gag, the ball itself is rubber and can be inflated, while with others the piece in the mouth is shaped like the head of a cock. This is the pecker gag, and is highly effective for submissive men, especially the advanced version, probably the kinkiest gag of all, in which the wearer holds the small dildo in his mouth and a larger one extends from the front, so that you can ride his head while he is gagged.

> With some gags, the mouth piece is in the shaped of the head of cock.

Another favourite, beloved by spanking enthusiasts, is the panty gag, in which people being spanked are made to take their own underwear in their mouths to keep them quiet. Head harnesses often include built in gags, including the most elaborate of all, the scold's bridle, a cage of metal and leather designed to fit snugly to the wearer's head, not only restricting speech but very obvious to other people.

Gags are easy to find from specialist suppliers, or to make unless you want something very elaborate. Leather is the ideal material, but rubber and cloth work perfectly well, while it's easy to find balls of the right size and type in any pet shop. I advise against using tape gags, but if you are going to, then test the tape on your own arm before using it on your partner and be very careful when taking it off.

Restraint

Most forms of bondage aim to make movement impossible, or at least severely limited, in order to create that helpless feeling which is so often central to the kink. If that's your thing a few domestic props are really all you need. Men's ties are useful, and add a nicely symbolic touch, also stockings, scarves, dressing gown cords, even curtain sashes, all of which will keep your partner in place if properly tied but also have a domestic touch that many people prefer to customised bondage gear. Their presence is also a lot easier to explain to Great Aunt Edith. Clothes-line is generally too rough for bondage, and string too thin.

With a little imagination most articles of clothing can be used for impromptu bondage.

With a little imagination, most articles of clothing can be used for impromptu bondage. The sleeves of a jumper can be pulled out and tied together, sometimes even wrapped around the body and knotted at the back like a straightjacket. Knickers can be pulled down and knotted

91

off to secure her legs. I've known women to wear ribbons in their hair so that their hands can be tied for sex.

Plenty of domestic items also make good props, and not only the bed. An ordinary, straight backed chair can be immensely versatile, especially if you like to combine bondage and spanking, while tables, banisters, door handles, taps and anything else to which a cord can be attached can be pressed into service. Some enthusiasts even customised their fixtures and fittings so that they appear innocent but can be put to use at the drop of a hint.

If you prefer your bondage gear made for purpose, then there are plenty of choices. Simple cuffs and straps can be purchased from high street sex shops, but these are seldom of very high quality and may be a bit jokey for some tastes. High quality equipment is less widely available, but easily purchased in specialist shops or online in a fairly comprehensive range of types and styles, although black leather with metal fittings remains the firm favourite.

The picture shows a set of birdcage handcuffs from Silken Ties, who specialise in high quality bondage equipment. They are made of chrome plated steel, which is both beautiful and effective. I took the photograph at the London Alternative Market, where I had a 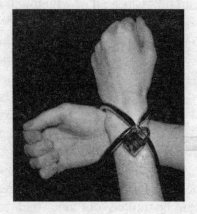 dozen or so different designs to choose from among almost as many different stalls.

In the unlikely event that you can't find what you

want, there are skilled people prepared to work to order, or you can always do it yourself.

Choice of material is important. Metal is highly effective and can look beautiful, but can be hard on the skin and awkward if you get into difficulties. After all, genuine hardened steel police handcuffs may be the only thing that enables you to live out that kinky police fantasy, but you're going to look pretty silly if you lose the key. The same goes for systems of chains and padlocks, but if that is your thing, make sure to number everything and keep it all together when not in use. Metal is also cold, which you may or may not regard as a good thing.

Leather cuffs and straps are effective and simple to use and also easy to cut if necessary. Strong, flexible and warm, leather also has a rich smell which many people find enjoyable, even essential. It is also easy to work and comes in a wide variety of colours and textures. Rubber has similar properties but is less durable and much harder to work.

Leather Work

Bondage gear can be expensive to buy, especially if you want it customised, so you may prefer to make your own. It's not difficult to find merchants for both leather and fittings.

A good hide should be thick and reasonably flexible. Too stiff and it may chaff, too soft and it may stretch, allowing easy escape.

A heavy duty craft knife is ideal for cutting, preferably on a wooden surface and against the side of a metal ruler. You will also need a leather punch and formers for riveting.

Choose cast or welded fittings made of brass or stainless steel, which are both strong and aesthetically pleasing. Fittings made of bent wire are seldom strong enough.

You may also want to purchase leather glue, although this should be used for finishing only, and not for joins that will be under tension.

Design and assembly is quite tricky and takes practice, even if you're naturally good with your hands. So be patient and practise on scraps before cutting into a full hide.

Other materials, such as artificial leather, heavy cloth and webbing can all be used effectively, but most serious bondage enthusiasts use rope.

Rope Bondage

Fastening a set of wrist cuffs is easy. Tying somebody's wrists together may look easy, but to do it well is another matter. The most important thing is to tie knots that don't slip, otherwise the ropes can tighten as you struggle, and bondage isn't nearly as much fun if you can't struggle. It is also important to choose the right sort of rope, not too thin nor too thick, and not too stiff nor too rough. What's right for you may not necessarily be right for others, but, broadly speaking, a good bondage rope should be 6 to 8mm thick and ideally made of cotton or hemp, although polyester and other man-made fibres are generally acceptable. As is so often the case with kinky accessories, you're likely to pay more if you buy from a specialist supplier. This is less true than for many areas, but be wary of inflated prices. Perfectly good rope can be bought at very reasonable prices from DIY stores and chandlers. Most ropes are plaited, and quite smooth, but some people prefer twisted rope, which has a deeper relief on the surface and therefore leaves distinctively patterned marks on your skin. Another good choice is magician's rope, which is designed for magic tricks. It is soft and hollow, so ideal for play unless you need the sensation of being heavily bound.

Perfectly good rope can be bought at reasonable prices from DIY stores and chandlers.

A two-metre length of rope is all you need to make an effective tie for wrists or ankles, while a four-metre piece will serve to secure your partner to the bed or fixture of choice. For a starter kit, I would advise four lengths of two metres and two of four metres, while a more advanced kit might consist of four lengths of two metres, four lengths of four metres, two lengths of eight metres and a single length of sixteen metres, which will allow you full scope for all but the most elaborate systems. If you are going to be tying systems in which two or more ropes overlap it is best to buy contrasting colours.

Having bought your rope, the first thing to do is seal the ends to prevent fraying. A twist of heavy duty tape will do this adequately, or you can use the traditional technique and whip the end with fine cord. Man made fibres can be heat sealed by melting the tip, but be careful not to leave any sharp edges. My own choice is to dip the ends into liquid latex, which dries to form a soft, durable bond ideal for purpose. To wash your rope, put it in the washing machine inside a pillow case.

I strongly advise practising your knots before attempting to tie anybody up, otherwise they're likely to end up laughing at you.

Once you have your rope I strongly advise practising your

knots before attempting to tie anybody up, otherwise they're likely to end up laughing at you while you struggle in a tangle of rope and then escaping in seconds,

none of which does much for that dominant poise. A rolled up towel makes a good practise limb or pair of limbs, as it's soft but won't go ouch when you make a mistake, or laugh at you.

You can use just two basic ties; one for attaching two limbs together and one for attaching one limb to a fixed object. For these, and for almost all other purposes, you need to learn two basic knots, the reef knot and the bowline (pronounced bow_lin). Learn these first and practise until you can do both knots with your eyes shut.

The reef knot is a simple and elegant knot designed to tie together two ends of a single line and is therefore ideal for knotting off ties fixing two limbs together.

Take a piece of rope and follow the diagram, making sure that the finished knot is symmetrical as shown. To tie a reef knot you need a make a

> The reef knot is a simple and elegant knot ideal for tying off bonds used to fix two limbs together.

left handed twist followed by a right handed twist, or *vice versa*. If your knot doesn't look right you have probably made two twists in the same direction, forming a granny

knot, which can slip if pulled hard and is often difficult to untie. There are a great many situations in which a reef knot should not be used, but this is a bondage manual and not a handbook for mountaineers, so all you need to know is that if you tie off a loop with a reef knot and then pull on the loop it will slip and tighten.

The second essential knot, the bowline, forms a secure loop, which will not slip no matter how hard you pull on it, making it ideal for tying a single limb which can then be tied to something else. The bowline is harder to tie than the reef knot, but by no means difficult. Follow the diagram and you'll soon have the knack.

As you can see in the picture, a bowline can be tied at the end of a line already secured to something else, allowing you to partially set up a bondage system in advance, or to keep the rope attached while you move your partner from one place to another, so that it is also the ideal knot to use when making a lead.

The disadvantage of a simple bowline is that there is only one line of rope around the limb, which can be uncomfortable. To get around this, you can use a French bowline, which makes three loops instead of one, distributing the pressure more evenly. The picture shows the first stage for a French bowline, with a triple loop instead of a single loop.

Tighten knots with your fingers rather than tugging at them, gently when first tied and then firmly once the bondage system is complete.

When completing the knot, be sure to pass the end over all three loops before tucking it back as shown in stage three for the simple bowline. Note that in all these pictures the rope is positioned so as to show the different stages used in tying the knots so that they can be followed easily and that you'll need to adjust the length used in practice. The rope is 12mm thick marine cord made of polyester, which is ideal for demonstrations of knotting, but too thick, stiff and rough to make good bondage rope.

When you are proficient with both knots you can move on to tying up. Once you decide to graduate from the two ends of your rolled towel to your partner, you need to be careful when tightening your knots. Never jerk or tug the rope tight, as if it's on bare skin the knot is likely to pinch. Tighten the knot with your fingers instead, gently after you first make it and then firmly

However carefully you've followed the safety rules, there's always the possibility of pins-and-needles or cramp, especially during active sex, while it's also possible you reach a limit for being tied up. to become to strong to handle.

98

once the bondage system is complete. Wrists are especially sensitive, and, if you're having yours tied, gloves make a useful barrier between the rope and your skin.

It's also important to be able to dismantle the system quickly. If your partner uses your safe word, untie him or her immediately, and keep a pair of cloth shears handy to cut the rope if need be. However carefully you've  followed the safety rules, there's always the possibility of pins-and-needles or cramp, especially during active sex, while it's also possible for your reactions to being tied-up to become too strong to handle.

A good system to start with is to tie your partner spread-eagled on a bed with each limb tied to a post. For this, you need four two metre lengths of rope, one to each limb. Tie both wrists and ankles as shown in the picture, which illustrates three different types of bowline tied to a gloved wrist with 6mm polyester cord, which is ideal for the purpose. The first tie is a plain bowline, the second a French bowline and the third a double bowline, which is tied exactly the same way as a plain bowline but with the rope doubled up so that instead of a loose end you get a loop. The loop can then be used to attach other ropes, as shown. The loose ends of the rope then attach to the bedposts.

A simple variation on this is to tie all four ropes to the posts at the head of the bed and use them to tie both wrists and ankles, leaving your partner rolled up.

If you want to tie his or her wrists or ankles together but not restrict movement completely, use a French bowline on each limb, leaving slack rope between, but if you want to tie any two limbs tight together you need to tie a cinch (pronounced sinch) which tightens the rope between the wrists and is essential for any tie that make a close join between limbs. As with the French bowline, it is important to make several loops around each limb in order to distribute the pressure of the rope.

The pictures show a three-turn cinch to tie Mikki's hands behind her back using two metres of 6mm rope.

1 – Place the rope behind her wrists.

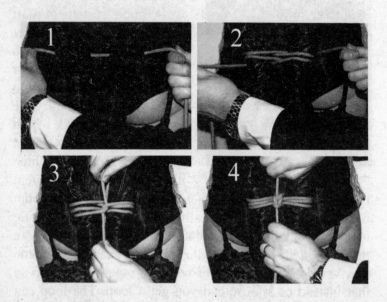

2 – Thread the rope around her wrists so that the strands cross in the middle.

3 – On the last twist, turn each strand of rope at right angles around the other.

4 – Wind both strands around the central section of rope, tighten and fix with a reef knot.

With your wrists tied in front of your body, it's usually

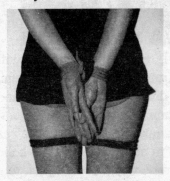

possible to escape by loosening the knot with your teeth, while even with your arms behind your back you may be able to get your legs up and pass the tie under your feet, if you're sufficiently flexible. The picture shows a simple way around this, with Mikki's wrists fixed behind her back and tied off to a second cinch around her thighs. She did eventually manage to escape, but only after a great deal of wriggling, which is as it should be for all but the most intense rope bondage ties.

To get the best out of bondage, it's important to feel you can't escape too easily, but you also need to be sufficiently comfortable to enjoy the experience. What's good and what's not is entirely personal, but a good, safe guideline when making ties is

Leave enough space for your little finger to fit between rope and skin.

always to leave enough space for your little finger to fit between rope and skin. That way your partner probably will be able to escape, in half-an-hour or so, but by then you'll have had your wicked way with him or her.

Bondage Positions

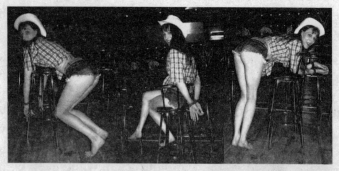

You now have the basics, and, with a little practice, will soon be able to put your partner in effective bondage. Bondage positions come in almost infinite variety, and it's possible to buy step-by-step guides showing several dozen positions which aficionados still criticise as insufficiently detailed. Here, I'm more concerned with the practicalities than with fancy rope work, so will stick to a few classics, all of which can be done with the ties already discussed. We've already looked at the Spread-eagle, which is simple, functional and ideal for restraint that leaves one side of the body vulnerable. The Spread-eagle is ideal for a four-poster bed, but a chair is much more versatile, allowing you to place your partner in a wide variety of useful and intriguing positions. For all three of the positions shown above, Sophie is fastened to the chair with a single two-metre length of 6mm rope either tied with a French bowline at either wrist or with a cinch fastening them together. These took a few seconds to tie and even less to undo. Without a prop, you need to tie different parts of the body to each other, which is a little slower.

The best-known bondage position of all is the Hogtie, long associated with the deep south of the USA. This can be simple or elaborate, but an effective Hogtie can be achieved with a single four-metre length of rope, as

shown in the picture.

Sophie's hands were tied behind her back first, the cinch tied off with a reef knot to leave enough rope to tie her ankles in the same fashion, with the ends again tied off with another reef knot. This is a loose Hogtie, with plenty of slack between her wrists and ankles, and she was comfortable for the half-hour or so she was tied up. A tight Hogtie, with the wrists and ankles bound close together, places strain on the chest and can quickly become uncomfortable. The disadvantage of a Hogtie is that the rope joining her wrists to her ankles made it difficult to get at her bottom.

The position shown at the beginning of the section is the Frog Tie, which mimics the way a frog sits. This was done with a single eight-metre length of 4mm polyester

rope. First, the rope was doubled up and fixed to the centre of a 15" spreader bar with a simple hitch, as shown. This left two equal lengths of rope which were secured to the eyelets at either end of the bar using reef knots. Each of Ivy's wrists was then tied with a double bowline and secured to her legs with cinches of four twists between her calves and thighs. The loose ends were fixed to the loops of the double bowlines to finish.

As you can see, the Frog Tie makes it almost impossible to move but also leaves you vulnerable, while Ivy stayed tied up for about half-an-hour without discomfort. That makes it an excellent position for play, especially on a bed.

Other positions emphasise feelings of helplessness or exposure, while some relate to particular cultures or fantasies. Most positions are symmetrical, but asymmetrical bondage can have a disorientating effect, making your body feel off balance and increasing the psychological impact of being tied up.

Body Harness

A body harness is any system of ropes which encases the body, whether or not it is also restrictive. This is a useful basic technique, both as a frame onto which further bonds can be attached, in some cases for restriction and in others for its own sake as the sensation of being tied and the pressure of the ropes can provide their own pleasure.

There are, effectively, a limitless number of different designs, depending on how

There are, effectively, a limitless number of different harness designs.

the ropes are placed and tied, while it is possible to make an effective body harness without using any knots at all. Some people use the Japanese term "karada", meaning body, and there are many subtle distinctions, both traditional and modern, between different types of harness. Most designs encase only the torso, but some include the legs and arms, while the great majority form a symmetrical pattern of ropes designed to be aesthetically pleasing as well as to produce distinctive patterns of pressure on the body.

The picture shows a harness tied with six metres of 10mm silk rope. Note that the loop is draped only lightly over her neck and that there is no danger of rope pressing on her windpipe. The loop was tied first, by doubling the rope and passing it back through itself, the simplest of knots. Another four of these, evenly spaced at roughly the width of your hand was used to form a double rope designed to stretch from neck to crotch. This was then draped over her neck, fed back between her legs and led up her body in a zigzag pattern, as shown, before being tied off in the middle of her back.

More complicated rope harnesses may include all four limbs and even your hair, while knots can be used to create plaques or buttons of rope at specific pressure points, or simply for decoration. In the harness shown above, the lowest of the five knots is positioned so that it presses to her clitoris as she moves, perhaps the most obvious use of a pressure point and also the most effective.

The simplest form of plaque is the Carrick Bend, which is similar to a Reef Knot and shown here loosely tied with two cords of contrasting colour in order to make it easier to follow. Larger plaque knots create a mat of rope, allowing pressure to be evenly applied across a considerable area. Plaque

knots should be tightened gradually and never tugged hard or you'll end up with rope spaghetti.

While plaques are flat and apply a low pressure spread over the area of the knot, rope buttons are round and apply considerably more pressure to a smaller area. The simplest is the Chinese Button, which is shown here made up loose with cords of contrasting colours in order to make it easier to follow, and also tied

tight. Using two cords also makes the button a better starting point for a body harness.

Unless you are proficient, the Chinese Button can be quite tricky to tie, so I recommend preparing it in advance. In order to get a Chinese Button at the centre of a piece of rope, first fold the cord to find the centre point, which you may want to mark. Place the cord on a flat surface and lay it out with the centre point at the middle of the pattern, then tighten gradually, making sure the two ends remain the same length. For a double cord, you might find it easier to lay out one cord in the above pattern first and thread the second alongside the first.

The Carrick Bend and the Chinese Button are only two among hundreds of similar knots, but if want to investigate further, I recommend the Ashley Book of Knots, which has over 4,000 illustrations and is known as the knot-maker's bible, at least for Western tradition.

Enclosure

A sufficiently elaborate body harness can give almost complete enclosure of the body, creating a new sensation; complete helplessness mixed with general pressure and a sense of being encased. A net achieves the same effect much more easily, and while you can make your own with a bit of practice, a football or tennis net serves most purposes. Nets can also be used for hunting games, but that belongs in a later chapter.

If you like the idea of full enclosure from feet to neck,

Clingfilm works well, and not only follows every contour of your body but is thin and transparent, allowing you to be naked and vulnerable to touch while still bound tight. It can also be broken easily, allowing your partner access to parts of your body. Commercial Clingfilm is wider and easier to handle, while industrial pallet wrap can be used the same way and is not only wider still, but tougher, stickier and available in a range of colours. Bindings should be firm rather than tight to avoid risk of cutting off circulation, and plastic sheeting should never be used to cover the head or in any way that blocks the airways.

For many people, bandages make the ideal body enclosure.

It is possible to buy purpose-made bondage tape and a wide variety of similar products, but for many people, bandages make the ideal body enclosure; soft, permeable to air and designed to purpose. Bandages allow complete mummification, although as always you need to be absolutely sure that your partner can breathe without difficulty and that there is no risk of him or her falling. The picture shows a bandage being put on, slightly stretched and overlapping to give a firm feel as her arms are bound to her chest. The end of the bandage should be tucked in to hold it in place.

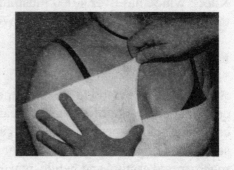

Complete mummification is a very intense sensation, more so than you might expect, creating a sense of absolute dependence, detachment and even feelings of well being and nurture. It is also the most comfortable form of bondage, but in some ways the most absolute, making it ideal for those who enjoy being encased and unable to resist, but dislike pain or awkward positions.

> Enclosure can be used to bind limbs for restriction, erotic humiliation or display.

Enclosure can also be used to bind limbs for restriction, erotic humiliation or display, especially to make you into a mermaid, or a human caterpillar for that matter, but again that belongs to a later chapter.

Predicament Bondage

Any situation in which being tied up puts you in an awkward situation can be called predicament bondage. The situation can be painful, frustrating, embarrassing, frightening, or any combination of the strong emotions you get with being in bondage, as it should be designed to make your feelings of helplessness and frustration more intense, and to provide enjoyment for your watching partner.

> Predicament bondage can be painful, frustrating, embarrassing, frightening, or any combination of the strong emotions you get with being in bondage.

The simplest form of predicament bondage is to tie somebody up in order to tease, as shown in the picture ovefleaf, which we recreated from an old 1920s postcard of a French girl teasing a German soldier who'd been tied to a tree. The clothes are different, but the poses are the same and the idea must be as old as the human race. It's also very simple and very effective, as while Mark's hands are tied

behind the tree with a simple cinch he was completely unable to escape, but it took only a few seconds to release him.

Another, rather crueller, form of predicament bondage is to tie your partner in such a way that he or she has a choice of two positions, both of which are uncomfortable, or perhaps so that it is possible to get more comfortable but not without consequences. For example, you might be able to tie your partner in the bath and have him or her hold a bit between the teeth in such a way that releasing it turns the shower on, full power and cold.

If you enjoy erotic humiliation, a simple but effective predicament bondage technique is to rig a system so that the only way to escape is to undress, as shown in the pictures below. Leia-Ann is tied between two trees, both well out of her reach, while the rope has been threaded through the belts loops of her jeans and tied off behind her back with a reef knot to keep her in the centre. Her hands are also tied

> If you enjoy erotic humiliation, a simple but effective predicament bondage technique is to rig a system so that the only way to escape is to undress.

in front of her in order to prevent her getting at the reef knot and to tempt her to open the button of her jeans and accept that to escape she would have to strip to her knickers and top. Of course, she could have opened the

cinch with her teeth first, loosened the reef knot and moved slowly along the rope until she could reach a tree, but that would have taken much longer. Why she chose to take her knickers off as well as her jeans I can only guess.

Outdoor Bondage

The great outdoors is full of opportunities for inventive bondage so long as you can guarantee privacy. For those lucky enough to have access to private land, all sorts of things can be put to good use – fences, gates, stiles, farm machinery, even old barrels and carriage wheels – but unless you feel the need to play out a specific fantasy, there's very little you can't do with a conveniently shaped tree. In the picture overleaf, Leia-Ann's hands are tied with a cinch, from which a rope leads over a forked branch to the trunk of the tree, on which it is tied off to

leave her vulnerable and almost helpless. Tying her feet together would have made her more helpless still, but made it difficult for her to balance, something you need to be especially careful of outdoors. You generally need more rope outdoors, if only because there's so much more space to use, but we found the 20m length of 10mm nylon cord awkward and could easily have done both this tie and the predicament bondage tie with half the length. Note that I used a softer, finer cord to tie her wrists as it was against her skin, while the much tougher nylon was better against the bark of the tree.

Unfortunately, most outdoor bondage fantasies are impractical for all but a few lucky people, but there is one that deserves a mention, being tied over the barrel of a canon for the old naval punishment called "kissing the gunner's daughter". Like most outdoor bondage ties, this is designed to leave you helpless, in this case for a dose of the cat-o'-nine-tails or a rope's end, although it would more usually be for sex.

> You generally need more rope outdoors, if only because there's so much more space to use.

Double and Group Bondage

If being tied up excites you, then it may be that the idea of

being tied to a lover is more pleasurable still. Not only are you in close contact, but because you cannot pull apart you have the added pleasure of shedding your responsibility, perhaps even being unable to stop yourself. The illustration is of a very simple tie, with each partner's wrists cinched together behind the others back and tied off around their waists, allowing them to touch each other's bodies but only so far.

The problem for many people is that to do this effectively you really need a third person to be in control, to tie you properly and to be there to release you quickly if there are any problems. One way it does work well is as a kinky party game, both to help people get over their inhibitions and as a potential forfeit.

Double bondage makes predicament bondage ties even more interesting, and challenging. If you're tied to somebody else, you have little choice but to co-operate. For example, had Leia-Ann been tied back to back with somebody else, both with their hands cinched around the other's waist their only means of escape would have been to undress each other.

The more people involved, the more fun you can have, and it's possible to create extraordinarily complicated group bondage scenarios, as well as coffles and people tied in such a way that they can be put to unconventional uses, most often as furniture.

Naughty Furniture

Having one partner act as furniture for the other is a popular D/s game that mixes well with bondage. The classic image is of a man on all fours used as a dominant woman's footstool, while she sits at ease, perhaps with a drink in one hand and a riding crop in the other. A pair of spreader bars fixed between his four limbs like the cross pieces of a table can improve this scenario, while with a flat board tied to his back he can become a low table at which she and her friends can take morning coffee.

To be used as a chair can be more satisfying still, as in this picture, in which our model's wrists and ankles have been tied off to a spreader bar in the shape of a capital I, keeping him in position as Sophie's stool while she enjoys a drink with a friend. It's sensible to have the stronger, heavier partner as the stool, so this is usually, and literally, a woman-on-top fantasy.

With a girl, when tied in a standing position and supported to prevent the risk of falling, she can make a useful and decorative hat stand, perhaps positioned in the hall for the use of your guests before a party. Or there's always the option of decorative statuary, in which case you'll need to expand your knowledge of knots and ties.

Advanced Bondage

At its most elaborate, rope bondage becomes an art form, in which elegance and structure are as important as restraint. Even to scratch the surface of the subject would take a book of its own, but several have been written, while it's also possible to attend workshops and demonstrations on bondage technique, so if you want to explore further there's plenty of opportunity. Much of this knowledge is based on Japanese rope bondage, generally known as Shibari or Kinbaku, which concentrates on aesthetics and the pleasure gained from the pressure of the ropes as much as on restraint. There are also European influences, especially sailor's knots, and doubtless others, but modern erotic bondage is now becoming international.

> There are several good books on advanced bondage technique, and you may also be able to attend workshops and demonstrations.

This is not something I am going to look at in detail, as it is simply too complicated, but to give an idea of what can be achieved the chapter finishes with an example of artistic bondage tied and photographed by Mark Varley of Beautiful Bondage. This shows influences from Japan and Britain. His model is tied into an arm bind that is both attractive and functional, using double strands of soft, plain hemp. The hitches down her arms provide anchor points and fasten her wrists together. Her hair is bound into pigtails from which the rope leads down her back, lacing her arms tight together to either side like a Carrick Hitches. The overall effect is elegant,

> The ideal of artistic bondage is to be both effective and decorative.

striking and also effective, keeping her securely in position and displaying the rope work to best advantage. To do this requires skill, knowledge and patience, but to my mind at least the beauty of the result justifies the effort.

Play Rooms and Equipment

For most of the people, most of the time, sex happens in the bedroom. Anything to do with sex also tends to belong in the bedroom, even if it's just a vibrator hidden at the bottom of the knicker drawer. If you enjoy kinky sex, you're going to need a little more, and if you're not content with making use of everyday items you'll soon find you have a collection of gear.

The chances are you'll need to be discreet, and while whips and chains can be concealed easily enough, furniture purpose built for sex play can take a little explaining. If that's not a problem for you, there's plenty of gear on the market; pillories, whipping stools, padded benches, even cages if that's your thing. Designs vary, but most items are either intended to put you in a comfortable position in order to have uncomfortable things done to you, or in a rude position to have rude things done to you. A visit to a fetish market or a browse through suppliers on the net will soon give you an idea of what's available and what will suit you best.

You may prefer to make your own equipment, in which case there are two important rules to follow; make it strong and use plenty of padding. Make the joints properly, welded if you're using metal and using screws or bolts rather than nails for wood. Also, make sure it can't collapse at an awkward moment. A whipping stool may seem easy to make as it is really no more than a large sandwich board with a padded top, but it is essential to brace the legs so that they can't close when you're bent over it, because whatever your lover is doing to you from behind, it's sure to make you push forward. For padding, I recommend at least four inches of polystyrene foam with a PVC covering fixed in place with furniture nails, a combination that looks smart and is both durable and easy to wash. Leather is smarter still, but be sure to buy a tough but reasonably flexible hide. Cuffs for the wrists and ankles can also be added and are best secured by short lengths of strong chain, also eyes to which rope can be attached but bear in mind that if an eye is to take any real weight, it needs to be a bolt fitting on a substantial piece of wood rather than just a screw.

Three pieces of less standard equipment:

Berkley Horse – a large, open frame that allows you to be whipped behind and teased from the front.

Bristle Pig – a trestle topped with bristly doormat material, ensuring an uncomfortable ride.

Queening Stool – a padded stool with a hole in the seat to allow you to sit in comfort on your partner's face.

If you're very clever, you may be able to build your equipment so that it can be mistaken for everyday items, but if you have a moderate amount of space and privacy, you might prefer to have a dedicated play room. That way you can decorate it to your own taste, have all your equipment in one place and keep everything you don't want others to see in a locked room. A cellar is always a good choice if you have one and especially if you want to create a dungeon atmosphere, but the cleverest play room I've seen was a converted attic reached by a retractable ladder so that it was completely out of sight and out of mind most of the time but could be made available in an instant if a party began to get interesting.

It may well be that you're not able to have your own equipment, let alone your own play room, in which case there's always the option of hiring one. There are plenty of spaces like the Barnet Bastille for hire, usually by the hour. A good one should not only have plenty of high-quality equipment but facilities to change, wash and perhaps eat. Some, such as Studio 21 in West London, even boast full bed and breakfast facilities, allowing you to play with complete privacy for as long as you like, climb into a comfortable double bed and restore yourself with bacon and eggs in the morning. This is their bondage wheel.

Blushing at Both Ends

Spanking and other Ouchy Things

Spanking –just the word is a rush for me, even to think it. Being spanked and dishing it out to others has been one of the greatest pleasures of my life; exciting, fulfilling and always fresh. Spanking is like wine, bringing pleasure that never fades, but grows with experience, and, like wine, there is always something new to be appreciated, some subtle nuance or clever innovation. I adore spanking.

Where there's kinky behaviour, there's spanking, more often than not, so I've included a lot of detail in this section which can relate equally well to others. Spanking is also the most highly developed of kinks, perhaps not as universally

> If you go in too hard, you can easily put someone off for life, but if you go in too soft, with any luck you'll have him or her begging for more.

appreciated as erotic display or as elaborate as bondage, but with a strong cultural resonance and more subtle nuances than any other, which is why this is the longest section.

Unfortunately, that cultural resonance can make it hard to accept spanking as erotic play. To somebody who sees it merely as an aggressive act, my attitude may seem extraordinary, even incomprehensible. A teetotaller might feel the same about wine, a blanket condemnation that lumps the enthusiast sipping at his glass of exquisite Claret in with the abusive drunk. In both cases, there is good and there is bad, but surely the sensible thing to do is to focus on the good?

Everybody should be able to enjoy a gentle spanking, if only as stimulation of an erogenous zone, but, as usual, what's going on with your brain is more important than what's going on with your body. If the situation is wrong, or you're set against it for some reason, then it won't be enjoyable, but if you come to it with the right person, at the right time, and with a clear mind, then it will be.

Beyond the simple physical level, there are myriad subtle variations on the basic theme. For most people, to spank somebody is an act of dominance. After all, even when it's no more than a pat on the bum to admonish a friend, there's no question that the one doing the spanking is the boss, or at very least wants to be the boss. To protest, or to return the pat shows that you want to redress the balance of your relationship with that person, but to accept it is an act of submission, if only to the possibility of further contact.

> There's no question that the one doing the spanking is the boss.

For enthusiasts, spanking is usually the definitive act of dominance, just as to accept a spanking is the definitive act of submission. That doesn't mean roles can't be exchanged, or that you are in any way unequal in any other context, but when you're over somebody's knee with your bare red bottom stuck up in the air, or *vice versa*, there's no question when it comes to who's in charge.

Among those who play games of dominance and submission, even the mildest sort, a smack on the bottom is so much an accepted gesture from top to bottom that spanking in one form or another will often be incorporated in other forms of sex play. Yet, there's far more to spanking than just dominance and submission. Both physically and mentally, the degree to which spanking is sexual, from pure pleasure at one end of the spectrum to pure punishment at the other. It can be used as exhibitionism, as a cathartic experience, to relieve stress, as a way to help with self discipline, to reinforce a role within a relationship, as a way of working out personal differences, as a gesture of submission for its own sake, simply as play between friends, as in the picture, or as any possible combination of these things.

The idea of punishment is often associated with spanking. For some people, this is a straightforward desire to atone for something they've done, although it's more likely to be overdoing it on the cream cakes than robbing the local bank. The resulting spanking may or may not be sexual, may or may not be pleasurable physically or mentally while it is happening, but it is desired and that's what matters.

More commonly, the need for punishment is openly erotic, although it may still be associated with some sin or fault, real or made up. This relates to the build up of adrenalin associated with anticipation of the pain and embarrassment of punishment, also the release of endorphins caused by physical punishment, especially by spanking, which also stimulates the genital nervous network and therefore becomes erotic. Punishment can also be used as an excuse for breaking our society's nudity taboo, adding the embarrassment of going with a bare bottom to what is already a heady cocktail of erotic stimuli.

Another, very different, reason to enjoy a spanking is as a release. After a hard day at the office, it can be sheer bliss, shedding all responsibility, all respectability and every other care of the working environment as you lie yourself across your partner's lap to have your bottom laid bare and smacked. The same goes for many other situations, where a brisk spanking can pick you up as well as any drink, before going out for the evening perhaps, or

before your guests arrive for a party – maybe even after they arrive, which is guaranteed to break the ice, although it might

A brisk spanking can pick you up as well as any drink.

not be such a good idea if the guests are your future in-laws or the vicar and his wife. Then again, who knows...

It would certainly be embarrassing, and that's another key element in almost every spanking situation. A few people are so liberated that they can enjoy being spanked without a hint of embarrassment, and fewer still if it's done bare, but, for the great majority, embarrassment comes with the territory. For some, it's an awkward side effect, for others a necessary part of their punishment, but, for most, it's part of the pleasure, although there's often a very fine line between what's good and what's not.

Sometimes the pleasure can be almost entirely separate from the act, so that it's not being spanked that's exciting, but the knowledge that you are going to be spanked or that you've been spanked. For some people, especially those who are aroused by the idea of being punished, that knowledge alone can be enough to keep them on an erotic high for hours, even days. The other

side of the coin is perhaps the finest spanking experience of all, because with a receptive mindset and enough skill and care from your top, the pleasure can become transcendent, taking you out of

For some people, it is possible to reach orgasm from spanking alone.

yourself to a state of erotic rapture close to orgasm but very different. For some people, it is possible to reach orgasm from spanking alone, but again you need the right mental and physical balance and to be handled skilfully.

To somebody who has never been spanked, all this may sound a bit far fetched, but to anybody experienced it will be familiar territory, so all I can do is suggest you give it a try. If you do, then approach it in a positive frame of mind, because as with almost any new experience, if you tell yourself that it's not going to work for you, then it most probably won't.

> If you tell yourself that it's not going to work for you, then it probably won't.

The pleasure of dishing out a spanking is a lot easier to take in. After all, you've got your partner's bare bottom to enjoy and you're doing something that's likely to leave both of you in urgent need of sex. What's not to like?

Seriously though, some people do have reservations; because they think of spanking as a violent act, because they don't like the idea of sexual interaction except as equals, perhaps because of the social background to spanking and to corporal punishment in general. To me, what matters is that it's an informed choice made between consenting adults, and so long as that remains in clear sight, it is perfectly acceptable behaviour. My only concession is to fair play, in that I believe that if I spank somebody it gives him or her the right to spank me and *vice versa*, but that is my own personal choice and very much up to the individual.

> What matters is that it's an informed choice made between consenting adults.

For every reason to be spanked, there is a corresponding reason to do the spanking, even if only in order to satisfy your partner's need. To me, it seems instinctive. Just as a nipple or a cock cries out to be sucked, so a bottom cries out to be spanked. It's what bottoms are for.

A bottom cries out to be spanked. It's what bottoms are for.

When you're doing it, you're the one in charge, and so it's largely up to you to make the experience as satisfying as possible, so most of this section will be written from the viewpoint of the top. Not all of it though, because the way you behave when you're on the receiving end can be important, but the art of spanking lies in the hands of the one dishing it out. Simply grabbing your partner, stripping his or her bottom and laying in may be fun, and there's a lot to be said for springing it as a surprise, for spontaneity, and for rough and tumble, but that's only one way of doing it among many. It may well be off-putting if you don't give a chance to let his or her feelings build up, or if you start too hard.

If you want spanking to become a regular and important element of your relationship, then it's essential that your partner finds it pleasurable and/or fulfilling, in whatever way. That means doing it in a way that satisfies *his or her* need, or if he or she has never tried it but is willing to experiment, then making it a positive experience, something associated with your feelings for your partner, love as well as lust, and — unless the need is for pure discipline —with sex.

A virgin bottom needs care and attention, because if you go in too hard you can easily put someone off for life, but if you go in too soft, with any luck you'll have him or her begging for more. This is particularly true with women, who tend to be more emotionally sensitive being spanked. So pace yourself, build up gradually, take plenty of time out to caress her bottom, maybe stroke her hair and cuddle her too, but, above all, make sure she knows that you appreciate the intimacy of what you are doing together. If she's experienced but it's your first time together, she's likely to know what she wants, maybe in great detail, but will probably want you to be in charge during the actual spanking. So talk about it first, preferably by sharing your fantasies, which is likely to leave you both ready for action.

One to one domestic spanking may well be all you need, but many people like to play out roles and develop scenarios to satisfy their personal needs. Very often it will be plain old rough and tumble with the loser getting the spanking, but classic combinations include riding mistress and stable boy, boss and secretary, teacher and pupil, matron and patient. Or you might prefer something a little different; a scene from Victorian times or the Regency perhaps, or even Santa Claus spanking a naughty elf.

If you're prepared to let other people join in, the situation offers even more delicious possibilities. The shame of being laid bare bottom across your partner's knee is so often a key ingredient in spanking pleasure, and that can be multiplied a hundred fold if it's done in front of somebody else, or, perhaps stronger still, by somebody else while your partner watches.

Involving other people in your relationship requires enormous trust and care, which I've already discussed, but many people find it surprisingly easy to separate spanking from other sexual activity. I've even known cases where one partner goes to a third party for the discipline he or she craves with the full knowledge of the other. As always, what matters is what works for you.

Spanking games at parties are always fun, and provide an excuse to indulge yourself without the complications of needing to ask specific people, while many people find it easier, or better, to take punishment as a forfeit than to have to ask for it or wait hopefully for it to be dished out. Any game can be adapted for spanking purposes, or for kinky purposes in general, and different levels of exposure and severity can also be used to add to the fun.

Whatever you do, unless you're devoted to the rough and ready technique, there's sure to be an element of ritual to spanking. This can be broadly divided into: anticipation and exposure, which often go together, application – the spanking itself – and aftercare.

Anticipation and Exposure

Never underestimate the power of anticipation. It can make a huge difference to the spanking experience, allowing your partners' feelings to build up slowly, for minutes, hours, even days, so that when the moment finally arrives their emotions will be far stronger than if they'd been given no warning. Most of this is psychological, but there is a physical element as well, because their bodies are sure to respond to their emotions.

Just telling people that they're going to be spanked is usually pretty effective, but there are a multitude of subtle variations on the game, limited only by circumstances and your imagination. Other mind games you can play include having them toss a coin to see if they'll be allowed to keep any clothes on, or roll a dice to decide how many strokes of the cane they are to receive. An old favourite is to send someone who is about to be punished up to the bedroom to lie face down on the bed with his or her bottom bare. Or, if you have plenty of time, sit him or her in a room with a clock, preferably one that ticks loudly or chimes the hours.

> Having him dress a certain way when he's due to be spanked works well as a way of keeping him firmly in mind of what's coming.

Having your partner dress a certain way when due to be spanked works well as a way of keeping him or her firmly in mind of what's coming. For example, if you insist that your girlfriend always goes without knickers before a spanking, or wears them under a skirt but rolled down to the top of her thighs, or has to put on a particular pair, that will quickly become associated with the experience and exciting in its own right. For boys, having to wear girls' knickers works wonders, especially if he's going to be spanked in front of somebody else.

> Make sure that she is constantly aware of her bottom, and what's going to happen to it.

Whatever technique you choose, the important thing is to make sure that your partner is constantly aware of his or her bottom and what's going to happen to it, which will maintain the right mood until the time comes.

> Give him a bar of chocolate. If he eats it, spank him for being greedy. If he doesn't eat it, spank him for being ungrateful.

There are plenty of other tricks to make the experience more intense. A favourite for those who enjoy punishment play is to make the spanking seem unfair, perhaps by awarding it for something you both know hasn't been done, or putting them in a situation where whatever choice they make will lead to the same uncomfortable conclusion. Give them a bar of chocolate. If they eat it, spank them for being greedy. If they don't eat it, spank them for being ungrateful. If they insist on sharing it, spank them for trying to be clever. Imagine how they'll feel the next time you offer them a bar?

Putting partners in a predicament is much easier if other people are involved. For example, give them the choice of being taken upstairs for a spanking on the bare bottom, or being allowed to keep their clothes on but being done in front of friends. If they choose to let the friends watch, but you want to be really unfair, take their knickers down anyway. You can also make them choose who is going to spank them and ask politely for it to be done, even beg. If you enjoy harder corporal punishment, then having to make the implement that's going to be used on you adds a whole new dimension to the game. The classic example is birching, which comes with

> Position, restraint, clothing, atmosphere, all make a lot of difference.

its own elaborate ritual, which we'll come back to later.

Next, your partner needs to be made ready, which is usually an important part of a spanking, and can be crucial. Position, restraint, clothing, atmosphere, all make a lot of difference to his or her feelings, to say nothing of more exotic possibilities, such as being led out in front of an audience who know what is about to happen. Most important of all is the exposure of his or her bottom, because for somebody about to be spanked, the simple act of having the bottom exposed

> The simple act of having her bottom exposed can be overwhelming.

can be overwhelming. The words "bare bottom" and "spanking" go together like "peaches" and "cream". Most people like to be laid bare in most situations, although it's always wise to watch out for exceptions. For a lot of people, it's not only important to be laid bare, but essential, even the key point in the entire ritual. So make it count.

A lot of the time your partner will be wearing trousers, especially men, so unless you intend to put him in a skirt first and you want to spank him in any position in which his legs will be so wide apart it will make it hard to take his pants down properly, you'll need to get him bare first. If so, perhaps have him do it himself, while standing in front of you, or have him put his hands on his head while you take everything down for him.

You might well want your partner exposed in advance anyway, to be given a chance to contemplate the indignity of his or her position before the actual spanking, as with the graffiti artist in the pictures at the

> Give her a chance to contemplate the indignity of her position.

beginning of this section. Imagine she's been caught defacing the wall, told off, then made to stand in front of her handiwork with her bottom bare before she's spanked.

Another favourite is to make exposure part of the spanking itself, so that they're fully dressed at the start, then with their underwear on show and finally bare bottom, with the smacks growing gradually harder between each revelation. Taken to its extreme, this can mean starting fully dressed and ending up stark naked, but many people feel that the experience is best with only their bottom exposed, "fit for purpose" so to speak, as with this messy nurse.

There are different ways to go about the act of exposure. One is the short, sharp shock, which is most effective with a girl in a miniskirt, or maybe with a boy in

a kilt. Up comes the skirt and down come the knickers, as fast as possible, so that one moment she's decent and the next she's fully bare, which gives a sharp jolt of emotion. Another way is to be very casual about it, matter-of-fact, as if the fact that having her bottom laid bare to the world is utterly unimportant, which should ensure that she feels exactly the opposite – that it's the most important thing in the world.

Sometimes it's better to tease, perhaps by telling her she can keep her knickers up and then pulling them tight between her cheeks so that it makes very little difference, musing aloud over whether to take them down with your hand already gripped in the waistband, or maybe promising to leave them up if she doesn't make a fuss over her spanking, then pulling them down anyway. Yet

another choice is to do it slowly but firmly, with the waistband still touching her skin so that she's aware of every inch of exposure. Even when her cheeks are fully on show there are still decisions to be made, such as whether her panties should be left around the top of her thighs so that she's spared at least the final indignity of having her vulva exposed, or taken right down, or even off so that she can kick her legs freely when the spanking starts.

These techniques are great fun for you as the spanker, and are designed to be as embarrassing as possible for your partner, but be careful of his or her limits. Some people love being bare, or simply don't care. For others exposure, and specifically exposure for spanking, can be a very powerful experience, in a way that you can't fully understand unless you get spanked yourself and feel the same way. He or she may even want to cry, and a safe word is essential if you want to fully appreciate this sort of experience. However well you know somebody, you aren't a mind-reader, – beware of making assumptions based on gender, because, in my experience, there is more variation among individuals than between men and women.

For some people, anticipation is the best part of the whole experience, but that doesn't mean they should be let off, because the whole purpose of anticipation is to build up to the main event, the spanking, which begins with choosing a good position.

> These techniques are great fun for you as the spanker, and are designed to be as embarrassing as possible for your partner, but be careful of their limits.

Over the Knee and other Spanking Positions

Over the knee, or OTK, as shown at the beginning of the chapter, is the traditional spanking position and the one most people prefer. To lie bare bottom across your partner's lap is deliciously intimate, vulnerable and yielding and no other position brings home what it means to be given a spanking in quite the same way. From the spanker's point of view, it gives excellent control, making it easy to hold you in place with your bottom not only fully accessible but highly visible.

To give partners an OTK spanking the first thing to do is decide where you're going to sit. A sofa is ideal for a lingering, erotic session, but if you want to bring out their submissive feelings, a chair is much better. That way you can hold them with their head hanging down and their hands braced on the floor or gripped to the legs of the chair. They'll be very aware of what they are showing from behind, but it doesn't hurt to tell them. If you are right-handed, you'll want their bottom stuck out to the right, and *vice versa* if you're left-handed.

With a man, you may want to consider whether you want to have his bare cock rubbing on your leg while you spank him. If not, adjust his pants or place a towel underneath him, but, one way or another, there's no escaping the fact that OTK is a very intimate position. I'm assuming he's already bare, but if you prefer to expose him once he's in position and he's wearing trousers, make sure the button is undone before you put him across your knee.

Men generally like women to be fully exposed, so once she's in position, hold her firmly but gently, with your arm around her waist and your elbow in the centre of her back, which will help to keep her in position during the spanking and encourage her to arch her back in order to make her bottom lift and open. Alternatively, hold one or both of her arms behind her back, which will leave her feeling even more helpless. To complete her exposure, raise your right knee slightly to bring her bottom into even greater prominence and make sure her legs are tucked under rather than stuck straight out, which will help her cheeks to open. This position should leave both her vulva and anus showing from behind.

A useful refinement to the position is to have her spread her legs across one of yours, which not only leaves

her completely exposed but means that as she is spanked she will be rubbing herself on your thigh. You can also place her across just one leg, leaving the other free to trap one or both of hers, keeping her securely in position, but still able to kick her free leg, a particularly

awkward situation to be in, as shown. Alternatively, tip her up higher still, so that so that her head is close to the floor and she has difficulty keeping her feet on the ground, an awkward position, but one that should bring her feelings of helplessness and exposure to a peak.

OTK is by far the most popular spanking position, but only one of many. All you really need to do is to get at your partner's bottom, but for erotic spanking all the best positions are both vulnerable and sexually provocative, such as crawling, kneeling on a chair, or as follows.

A few of the classics:

Bedtime Spanking – face down on the bed with a pillow under the hips. Better than a cup of cocoa.

OTS – slung over the shoulder, bottom to the front.

Gym Discipline – legs braced apart, hands holding the ankles or resting on the knees. Hard to stay still.

The Diaper Position – lying down, legs held up as if having a nappy changed. Exceptionally embarrassing.

Turned Turtle –rolled right up, knees to either side of your head. Even more embarrassing, if possible.

The Potato Sack – Held under one arm, bum to the front.

Horsed Up – held by the hands and lifted onto somebody's back. Takes three, but hey...

The Brat – stood up straight, hands on the head.

The Awkward Brat – a handstand, held up by the ankles.

The Loser – face down on the floor, sat on.

The Open Bailey – face to the floor, bottom up, legs wide across your partner's thighs as he or she relaxes on the sofa. Named after Spanking Queen, Lucy Bailey, and a great position to mix in some more conventional sex.

The Spanking

OK, so your partner is ready for spanking. In this case, *her* knickers are down and she is trembling with anticipation. You have your target...
...but where should you aim?

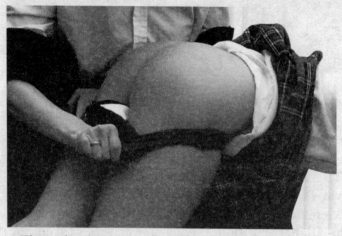

The only absolute rule is to go for the fleshy bits and avoid the bony ones. Never smack higher than the top of the bottom crease, where the bones of the sacrum and coccyx lie close under the skin. The harder the swat, the more important this is, so if you are using an implement, always aim for the fleshiest part of the bottom. Aside from that, it's a question of what effect you want to produce and the balance between pain and erotic sensation. The backs of the thighs sting but don't feel particularly sexy, so make a useful target when it's a punishment spanking or perhaps when your partner is daring you to do your worst. Smacking the sides of the hips produces a duller, heavier sensation, but again not particularly sexual.

The cheeks are the prime target, sensitive and sexual,

especially the lower part, the sweet spot, where they tuck under to either side of the anal area. Spank the sweet spot and every smack sends a jolt to the anus and genitals, not only by giving as much pleasure as possible for the pain but also maintaining awareness of the sexual nature of what you're doing. With men, it's best to check if he enjoys having his balls smacked.

The cheeks are the prime target, sensitive and sexual, especially the lower part, known as the sweet spot.

The simplest technique is to use the flat of your hand full across both cheeks, with a constant force and to a regular rhythm; a good, old fashioned spanking. It hurts at first, which makes it hard for her to keep control, both mentally and physically. Her endorphins won't kick in properly for some time, so it works well as a punishment, or as foreplay when it's not intended to lead directly to sex.

For a more immediately erotic spanking, you need to start slowly and pay more attention to her bottom. Expose her gradually, start gently and build up, varying your technique. Pats are nice, painless but pleasurable and intimate, so ideal if it's her first time or she's nervous about the pain. Using just the tips of the fingers produces a sharp, stinging sensation and allows the smacks to be delivered precisely on target, a good technique when you want to warm her cheeks all over before getting down to business. Smacking with the flat of your hand produces a duller, heavier sensation, the classic spanking feeling. Cupping your hand makes the smacks louder, useful if you want other people to hear

For erotic spanking, you need to start slowly and pay plenty of attention to her bottom.

what's happening, at a party for example, when you might take your partner somewhere private for a spanking but want to be sure that she knows other people can hear what's happening even if they can't see.

Cupping your hand makes the smacks louder, useful if you want other people to hear what's happening.

With new partners, it can be hard to judge what they want purely from their physical reactions. Some people make a fuss, others don't. Some like to struggle and swear, others to lie still and serene. It doesn't necessarily relate to how much they're enjoying themselves, so respond to their body language as best you can and always be ready to back off a little if need be. When you're on the receiving end, bear in mind that many spankers like you to wriggle and squeal, because it shows that they're getting their point across. Don't overdo it though, because if they think you're mocking them you'll be in bigger trouble than you already are.

A punishment spanking is best delivered as just that and nothing more; firm, no nonsense, without unnecessary touching. Otherwise, enjoy yourself, because any woman who'll let you spank her probably won't mind being stroked as well, whether simply for physical pleasure or to add to the humiliation of her situation, and with men this is doubly true. As the spanking proceeds you can grow gradually more intimate, within the boundaries of the relationship between the two of you and according to circumstances. It doesn't do much for your dominance to constantly

As the spanking proceeds you can grow gradually more intimate.

ask if you can go a little further, so it's best to do what you want and allow your partner to use a safe word if necessary, while with a regular partner you'll quickly learn to read his or her responses.

Some people can achieve orgasm through spanking alone, but most require a helping hand.

> Some people can achieve orgasm through spanking alone. Most require a helping hand.

As you spank, judge how your partner is reacting, in particular the balance between pain and pleasure, squeaks or sighs. Ideally, you want both all the way to climax. Hold on tight when the moment arrives and continue to spank, hard. You'll know when you're expected to stop, which is the perfect time for a cuddle, but that's aftercare, which comes later. First, the rough stuff.

Implements

If you want to explore spanking more fully, there are plenty of implements to play with; paddles, straps, switches, canes, whips and more, all of which can be as much fun as they are scary. With few exceptions, these hurt a lot more than a hand, and so should be used with care. My advice, although deeply unpopular with traditionalists, is that before you try it on somebody else, you should know how it feels yourself. That way you are better able to judge the effect of what you are doing, and the sort of sensations you're giving, which vary a great deal.

> Some implements are hard to handle, and it's best to practise on a cushion lightly dusted with talc before you use them on your partner.

Even the most ferocious of implements can be used gently, and as with hand spanking it's not just a matter of thrashing away blindly. A skilled user lets

141

the implement do the work and never needs to use the full

Warm up – A spanking given in advance of a more severe session.

strength of his or her arm. It's also a good idea to warm partners up with a brisk hand spanking before using an implement, because as their arousal increases they will be able to take more.

Some implements are hard to handle, and it's best to practise on a cushion lightly dusted with talc before you use them on your partner. The talc allows you to see where your stroke lands. This is especially important with longer and more flexible implements. It's also important to watch what you're doing. Always know where the tip of your implement is and make sure there's enough space around you if you have an audience. Stay sober.

Paddles

A paddle is any hard, flat object that can reasonably be applied to your bottom. Because they're rigid and broad, the surface of the paddle impacts with your flesh with a heavy, pushing sensation which suits the word "spank" to perfection.

Different sorts of paddles suit different situations; a ruler or gym shoe for college, a wooden spoon for the kitchen or dinner party, a hairbrush for the bedroom, all of which can be more or less real but share the domestic feel that many prefer to more overtly fetishistic scenarios. Customised paddles come in every shape and size, from small but surprisingly effective ones designed to be carried in a handbag or a pocket and applied when necessary, to impractically huge ones better suited to decoration than use.

My pet favourite is an old-fashioned clothes brush, designed like a hairbrush but longer and with stiff, densely packed bristles. Not only is it guaranteed to get a response out of even the toughest bottom, but the bristly side can be used to tickle and tease, while the long, rounded handle is perfect for insertion into one hole or another in order to finish the spanking off in style.

The heavier the paddle the more effective it is, but even a ruler can hurt. A big paddle carries a lot of energy  and can easily cause bruising, so go easy and do try a few swats on yourself before wading in. Large, wooden paddles are to the US spanking scene what the cane is to the British, and they have created an iconic fetish image with the "frat paddle", as used in college "hazing" rituals, in which a new member has to take a paddling at an initiation ceremony in order to get into a fraternity house, or a sorority house for girls. How common these rituals actually are is debatable, but it's a compelling image and that's no surprise. Imagine how John Boy feels knowing his sweet Peggy-Sue is over at the sorority house, skirt and panties off as she prepares for the application of the sorority paddle to her bottom, wielded by her equally cute friends in a ritual from which he is firmly excluded.

Using a paddle is easy, as they're short and rigid, but because they are hard and often heavy they are really only suitable for use on the bottom or perhaps the upper thighs, never on any part of the body where the bones are close to the surface. All but the largest paddles can be used effectively with your partner over your knee, and they are a popular way to finish off a hand spanking.

> All but the largest paddles can be used effectively with your partner over your knee, and they are a popular way to finish off a hand spanking.

Paddles can also be made from leather, rubber, plastic or any other reasonably stiff material, each of which has its distinctive feel. Some are ridged or set with studs, others have holes or fur on the back so that you can be alternately spanked and tickled. Be careful that the edges are smooth, especially with wooden paddles, and always strike with the surface of the paddle flat on the flesh of the bottom.

A great many designs of paddle are available for purchase, but if you're not content with domestic implements and don't want to buy custom made equipment they are easy enough to make yourself, especially from wood.

> Some paddles have fur on the back so that you can be alternately spanked and tickled.

Start with a flat piece of hardwood, not pine because it splinters too easily, draw out the shape you want and cut it free with a fine toothed saw. Apply sandpaper until the wood is perfectly smooth, perhaps bind the handle with string to improve the grip or add some suitable decoration

– one paddle confiscated during a police raid in the 90s had the words "Wanker Spanker" painted on it, which must have been highly amusing when it became an

exhibit in court. Finally, oil or varnish the wood to keep it in good condition. Leatherwork is discussed elsewhere, and allows you to make much more elaborate designs. The one in the picture is an "armadillo paddle", made with overlapping strips of stiff black leather built up around a central spine of tough but flexible plastic, riveted together and studded on the upper surface. Needless to say, you do the spanking with the flat side!

Straps

Like paddles, straps are broad and flat, but they are also flexible. This makes them harder to use and practice is essential, especially with heavy examples. Generally, straps produce a heavy, stinging sensation, different to that of a paddle, but less sharp than a cane.

A belt is the commonest form of strap, crude but effective, with a rather masculine flavour. More stylish is the Scottish tawse, as modelled by Ivy in the picture, which came from Quality Control and cost around £50. It is made of thick, supple leather said to have been taken from the hide of a 30-year-old bull. It is exceptionally supple and heavy, which makes it very

> Straps are hard to use and practice is essential.

145

effective but difficult to use, while a stiffer tawse would be easier but less satisfying.

A typical tawse is 18 inches to two feet long, with one end sculpted to form a handle and the other split into two or three tails. Most custom made straps are based on the tawse and many different designs exist, but thick, supple leather is the mark of quality.

Because of its flexibility, a strap will tend to drop if it is applied horizontally, and most straps are too long to be used effectively with your partner over your knee, so the best position in which to take a strapping is to lie face down on your bed, perhaps with your clothing adjusted to leave your bottom bare but protect your back and thighs. That way, the strokes can be applied vertically, but the wielder still needs to take care to aim properly. A good stroke should never wrap around to the hip, so the tip of the strap should be aimed three-quarters of the way across the far buttock. When you can lay a dozen strokes in a row on a talc-covered cushion without once allowing the tip of the strap to fall beyond where you're aiming, then you are ready to giving a strapping, not before.

If you do want to use the strap with your partner standing or bending over, then practice is even more important. The knack is to use both hands, one to apply the strap and the other to guide the stroke. Aim first, standing behind and to the side in such a way that the natural swing of your arm will bring the tip of the strap three-quarters of the way across his or her far bottom cheek. Duck down a little to make sure the strap lands horizontally. Grip the handle of the strap in one hand and let the tails slide through the other hand as you deliver the stroke, thus guiding them accurately onto target. You'll soon get the knack and be able to use the strap to a smooth, even rhythm. If you choose to practise with a pillow first and your partner finds this amusing, well, you know what to do.

> The knack is to use both hands, one to apply the strap and the other to guide the stroke.

The tip of a strap will always strike hardest, so to keep the impacts evenly distributed across both bottom cheeks you will need to swap sides if your partner is lying down, and to learn a backhanded stroke if he or she is standing or bent over. If you alternate between cheeks, it will make the strapping slower and more intense, as your partner will be aware of exactly what's coming next.

Being supple, a strap can also be used on your legs and on the palm of your hand, which makes them versatile for role-play scenarios. Because

of the Scottish origins of the tawse, they go well with college discipline scenarios. A girl can offer a very tempting target in a tartan miniskirt, or maybe best of all, a boy in a kilt but nothing on underneath.

Canes

The cane is the precision instrument of the corporal punishment enthusiast, with a very English feel and an austere elegance all its own. Long, thin and moderately flexible, a cane requires considerable skill to use properly and produces a very different sensation to paddles and straps; sharp and biting.

> The cane is not a beginner's implement. If you want to play, work up to it.

A cane is technically a section of stem from any woody, jointed grass, but in practice, canes designed for corporal punishment are nearly always rattan from the genera *Freycinetia* or *Calamus*. Bamboo is too brittle and tends to splinter, so should be avoided. Kooboo is the one most commonly used, making a light, flexible cane, while Dragon is darker, heavier and a little stiffer, allowing greater accuracy. Malacca is excellent but hard to find. Similar implements made of other materials such as fibreglass, steel and very rarely whalebone are not strictly speaking canes at all, but the distinction seems pedantic when one is being applied to your bare bottom.

A straight cane shaft can easily twist or slip in your grip, so they are generally either given a crook handle, the classic college style, or a grip of leather or rubber. A typical cane will be

> Six-of-the-Best Six hard strokes with any implement, but usually a cane.

one quarter to one half of an inch thick; any thinner or any thicker and they become unwieldy and potentially dangerous, although very thin canes can be used in a bunch. Crooked handled college canes are usually made from yard- or metre-long lengths, but many are a great deal shorter. A good cane should always have the tips and joints sanded down so that there are no sharp edges. They may also be oiled to keep them supple.

Using a cane well is an art, so much so that competitions are held to judge style and accuracy, such as the annual caning competition at The Firm's "Night of the Cane". When learning, start with a short, straight cane, no more than two feet long, first with a talc-covered cushion before graduating to your partner's bottom. This will let you develop your aim while the two of you explore the sensations your implement can provide.

> A good cane should always have the tips and joints sanded down so that there are no sharp edges.

Once you've mastered the short cane, you can move on to longer ones, and take it from me, practice makes perfect.

Even a light cane stroke will leave a faint pink line on the skin, so it's easy to see how you're getting on. As always, the important thing is that the cane should land on the bottom, not wrapping around to the hips and never hitting the back, while if you hold the cane at an angle you have to be careful not to hit the thighs. Experienced caners generally prefer neat,

> Five Bar Gate – A pattern of five evenly spaced horizontal lines with a sixth laid across diagonally, made with a cane on a subject's bottom. Not easy to do.

parallel strokes, weighted evenly across the cheeks, so that a traditional six of the best appears as six lines, all the same length and evenly spaced across the crest of her bottom. A real expert can produce what's called a "five bar gate", five parallel lines with the sixth laid diagonally across the others.

As with a strap, when giving a caning you should stand behind your partner and to the side, so that with your cane extended the tip touches three-quarters of the way across the far bottom cheek. A couple of taps will help to make sure you've got the line right, not to mention adding to his or her sense of trepidation. To apply a flat stroke you should either put all the action into your wrist or cane with your forearm bent. The more of your arm and body you put into the stroke, the harder it is to control.

Bent over is the traditional position in which to take the cane, as that leaves your bottom well presented and at a sensible height. It's not easy to stay still while it's being done, so while the gym discipline position looks good, you'll probably want something to hang on to, a desk or chair perhaps, or to be tied up, all of which can then become part of the ritual. Purpose built equipment such as a whipping stool or a pillory has the disadvantage that visitors are likely to notice if you leave it lying around the house. It can also be awkward visiting the swimming pool or beach in your new bikini when your bottom is decorated with half-a-dozen neatly laid cane stripes. Explanations can be tedious.

A caning is an extremely intense experience, and all

the more so if you make an elaborate ritual of it, using the full sequence of anticipation, exposure, application and aftercare. Even a straightforward domestic caning will be far stronger if you're told what is going to happen well in advance, made to dress to please or perhaps go naked for an hour beforehand, led to the sofa and made to kneel in position, exposed behind, warmed up with a sound spanking and finally six-

Imagine giving a dinner party at which your guests know that the after dinner entertainment is you; kneeling in your chair at the end of the table as your clothes are disarranged and six firm cane strokes applied to your bottom.

of-the-best while counting each stroke as it falls. If you have the right sort of friends, the idea can be taken a step further. Imagine giving a dinner party at which your guests know that the after dinner entertainment is you; kneeling in your chair at the end of the table as your clothes are disarranged and six firm cane strokes applied to your bottom.

The cane is ideal for role play, such as the college scenario, with a stern headmaster giving six-of-the-best to a defiant head girl, or perhaps a black-clad housekeeper administering a dozen strokes to an unruly footman.

Both the scenarios above are real, which for some people is essential. Others prefer role play, such as the college scenario, with a stern headmaster giving six-of-the-best to a defiant head girl, or perhaps a black-clad housekeeper administering a dozen strokes to an unruly footman. Both scenarios have the added thrill of dressing the part to give or receive punishment, and the clothes shopping can be a lot of fun as well, especially if whoever's going to be on the receiving end is sent out to buy the clothes in which he or she will be caned.

My personal favourite is Victorian role play, because not only does the severity and sexual hypocrisy of the age add to any scenario, but the clothing is wonderful, full and elaborate, so that exposure becomes far more meaningful than with modern clothes. The girl in the picture would already have had her dress, boots and three or more petticoats removed to leave her as she is, in stockings, a corset, chemise and split-seam Victorian drawers, kneeling on her bed with the cane held across her bare bottom as she awaits her punishment.

Switches

Switches are the simplest of implements and no doubt the first sort to be used on offending bottoms. Any suitably shaped shoot or twig will do and no doubt has at some time or another, but some are definitely better than others. The suckers that grow up around the trunks of many trees, such as apple, pear, sycamore and ash, are ideal. They should be cut when about a metre long and can be put to use straight away, singly, as a plait of three, or in a bunch. Handling this sort of switch is much like handling a cane,

> Switches are the simplest of implements and no doubt the first sort to be used on offending bottoms.

and they can be just as severe, if not more so, so take care.

Willow fronds make a light, stingy switch, but are almost impossible to keep on target, so best employed for mild, outdoor play rather than punishment play. Some people use stinging nettles, which are covered under sensation play but they're not particularly effective for whipping as such, while there is a risk of an allergic reaction. The pain is sharp and exhilarating at the time, but the effects can last for days.

The classic switch is the birch rod, which consists of a bundle of twigs a metre or more long bound at one end to form a handle. Birching has a ritual all its own, ideal to bring out your feelings, so that you'll be apprehensive, sulky, embarrassed and more, helping to build your excitement for hours before your punishment. There are endless variations, and it's best done in the spring when the twigs are supple.

On the morning of your birching, tie a ribbon in your hair.* Go out into the woods and choose a birch tree with plenty of foliage.

*

Even if you're a boy. Go on, do as you're told...

153

There are plenty around, although Leia-Ann and I had to walk the best part of a mile before we found a suitable copse to take the picture.

Bind the first third of the twigs with your hair ribbon, making the bases of the twigs into a handle and leaving the bushy piece as the business end.

Once you've found your tree, cut twelve birch twigs, each about a metre long, and gather them into a bunch. Bind the first third of the twigs with your hair ribbon, making the bases of the twigs into a handle and leaving the bushy piece as the business end. Take the birch home and present it to whoever is going to punish you. If he or she is impressed it will be accepted, otherwise you will be sent back to make another and awarded extra strokes.

When the time comes, maybe that evening, present yourself for punishment. Girls should wear a loose dress with nothing underneath, easy to take off. Maybe boys should, too. You will be stripped and your hands tied then raised above your head with the rope tied off to leave you helpless to the birch. You will be tickled, teased, and finally get your bottom whipped. When you are done, you will be made to kiss the birch, then be released.

Birch produces a hot, sharp prickling sensation, deliciously erotic if done gently.

Birch produces a hot, sharp prickling sensation, deliciously erotic if done gently but quickly becoming painful when more force is applied. Birch twigs are jointed and quite rough, hence the prickly sensation, but if you use a birch too hard it is easy to break the skin, so apply it with skill and affection rather than just thrashing away. The twigs are light, so can be used anywhere on the body except the head, so long as you're gentle.

Whips

It's not easy to define exactly what is or is not a whip, save that they're long, thin and designed to get the attention of whoever's on the receiving end. Whips can be almost rigid — like riding crops – or flexible, have many tails – like floggers – or just one. They can vary in size from tiny, delicate creations designed to tease your nipples to monstrous things forty feet long. Really big whips require a great deal of skill to use at the best of times and are too severe for erotic play, so I'll stick to the practical stuff.

Riding crops are similar to canes, but are better used so that only the sting makes contact, which allows for a very precise whipping and also plenty of teasing in-between strokes. This makes them ideal for full on fetish scenarios and for use in a play room, as illustrated by Joanna and friend in the Barnet Bastille.

Full riding gear and a crop makes for a classic dominant image; haughty and cruel at the same time, also very smart, while you can walk anywhere but the centre of a city and nobody bats an eyelid (except for hunting saboteurs, which has been known to be a problem). Riding whips are also the implement of choice for pony-play, which we'll come to later.

Floggers are very different. They are used more like a strap than a cane, but are more flexible still, so it's important to keep the lash moving to hit your target. As with straps, a flogger can be guided through your spare hand, applied forehand or backhand, or used in a figure-of-eight motion so that only the tips make contact with the skin. Floggers can be the most sensual of spanking implements, especially if the tails are made of suede. These give a heavy, soft impact and can also be used to caress and tickle, making them ideal for a warm up, while if wielded carefully they can be used almost anywhere on the body. Having your chest whipped with a small suede flogger is a delightful experience, and in skilled hands, with a receptive partner, a soft flogger can be used on male or female genitals to the point of orgasm.

> Floggers can be the most sensual of spanking implements, especially if the tails are made of suede.

Leather tails give a sharper sensation, rubber sharper still, but can still be used on the back and legs with moderate force. The cat-o'nine-tails, made with braided rope, can look impressive but is really too severe for more than middle-weight application to the buttocks. Floggers also need to be aimed carefully or the tails will wrap around the hip, so as always, practise first and make sure you know how your implement feels.

> In skilled hands, with a receptive partner, a soft flogger can be used on male or female genitals to the point of orgasm.

Single tail whips, generally made of plaited leather, are perhaps the most elegant of all implements, but they are certainly the hardest to use. Even a small single tail can hurt as much as a cane, while

156

they are notoriously difficult to keep on target. However, they're also very versatile, and can be flicked or used bent double, even to bind the wrists; as well as being beautiful. Bigger single tails are really for show only, although a skilled demonstration can be very impressive.

> If you want to use big whips, find an expert to teach you first, and even then be extremely cautious.

There are many minor variations on the basic theme of a whip, such as the quirt, which has a double sting, or the coach whip, which has a long shaft and a relatively short lash, all of which can have their place in the right scenario, but my general advice remains the same: if you want to use them, find an expert to teach you first, and even then be extremely cautious.

Whips are harder to make than most other implements, but if your leather working skills are good enough it's possible to get some beautiful results, customised to your own needs. There are also several excellent whip makers around, but it's slow, difficult work and their products are not cheap.

The Weird and the Wonderful

The five categories above cover most implements, but there are a few that don't fit in which deserve a mention. Some are everyday household items, such as a wet towel, ideal for flicking at carelessly exposed bottoms, or a remote control for those little domestic disagreements about what to watch on TV. A bath brush makes an excellent, if rather heavy duty, paddle, and you can add to the experience with a good scrubbing in-between smacks during a bath-time spanking. Books also make remarkably effective paddles, while a rolled up magazine or newspaper is just the thing for an impromptu spanking.

Two excellent household items that are sadly no longer easy to find are the horse-hair fly whisk – perfect for a long, slow session of whipping, flicking and tickling  while your partner is tied and helpless – and a pet favourite of mine, the carpet beater, which you might think was strictly for domestic Victorian fantasy, but is one of the best implements around for gentle spanking, producing a light but sharp sensation that covers the whole bottom. I found the one Ivy is showing off in a junk shop for a few pence, but is well made and still serviceable. The few modern ones I've seen were inclined to splinter.

The rope's end is another largely forgotten implement; a short length of rope, often spliced, used as a whip. A hank of rope has a very similar effect. Sports kit such as oars, cricket bats and even tennis rackets are sometimes used for spanking, generally in initiation rituals, but they're all too large and clumsy to make effective implements for erotic spanking. Still, I suppose the idea of losers of tennis matches having to bend over the net to be bared and spanked with their opponent's racket is sexy, but I bet they'd kick you out of the club.

There are also various implements that are far too severe for erotic purposes, except to show off or to tease. A bull's pizzle is a whip made by stretching and twisting a bull's penis, then allowing it to dry in the sun. The result is grotesque, but I suppose being punished with a dried penis might be erotically symbolic. The sjambok is a ferocious whip traditionally made from rhinoceros or hippopotamus hide, sometimes even as a giant pizzle.

I suppose being punished with a dried penis might be erotically symbolic.

Then there are spanking machines, which really do exist. Most have a padded seat to bend over and an implement of some sort attached to an arm, although one clever design I have seen involved a converted exercise bike and a system of chains and cogs so that as you pedal you spank yourself. Most are electric. I suppose being put on one for a punishment would have a sort of mechanical inevitability about it, but, for me, most of the pleasure comes in interacting with other people. Although the idea goes back to Regency times, maybe earlier, most designs clearly never got beyond the drawing board. Nevertheless, a surprising number of modern designs are available for sale, at a price.

Quick Guide to Severity

Purrrr!
Furry paddles, suede floggers, horse hair whisk.
Ooo!
Hand spanking, small paddles and straps, leather floggers.
Ouch!
Most paddles and straps, the cane, switches, riding crops and small whips.
Oh no you don't!
Heavy canes, very large paddles, most whips.

Six Implements

Reading from bottom left to top right:
1 – Furry backed paddle
2 – Tawse style leather strap
3 – Hazel twig switch
4 – Leather handled cane
5 – Suede Flogger
6 – Short, braided leather single tail whip

Refinements

Spanking is always more fun with a few added touches to make the experience sexier, more intense, more embarrassing and generally more memorable. Simplest of these is to have plenty of interaction. Talk to your partner, either to turn him or her on, for the embarrassment or both, according to your needs as a couple. Dirty talk should come easily to partners, given the position they're in, or they can be told they've been naughty and thoroughly deserve what they're getting, pointing out how silly and rude they look with their red bottom stuck up in the air and everything showing from behind, telling them what will be done once you've finished. Make them talk too, maybe apologise for their behaviour or explain themselves – not easy during a spanking. Have them beg for their spanking, thank you for punishing them, or most popular of all, count the smacks, a cruel little game with a thousand subtle variations that is guaranteed to have them seething with frustration and feeling that it's just not fair. For example, give them six firm smacks but make the seventh a gentle pat. If they call out the number, tell them you were only aiming and you'll have to start again, but if they don't call out the number, tell them they've missed one and you'll have to start again. It isn't fair, but that's half the fun. All of this will make the experience stronger, adding confusion,

> Give him six firm smacks but make the seventh a gentle pat. If he calls out the number, tell him you were only aiming and you'll have to start again, but if he doesn't call out the number, tell him he's missed one and you'll have to start again.

panic, a sense of injustice or contrition, all sort of emotions, and all on top of the pain and the shame of being spanked in the first place.

If you're on the receiving end, you may not want to put up with this, in which case you can play the brat, teasing your partner into dishing out the spanking in the first place, then giving him or her back-chat while it's being dished out. If you can handle it, perhaps try stifling a yawn as he or she is putting every ounce of their strength into applying a hand to your bottom. Inevitably, this will mean you get a dose of the hairbrush instead, or even the cane, but that's really the whole point. Bratting is definitely for those who can take their medicine and like it, but it's fun and often hard to resist.

Playing the Brat – Giving your partner back-chat while you're being spanked.

More physical refinements include bondage, which is dealt with in detail elsewhere but deserves a mention, and erotic humiliation, which for many people is inextricably linked to spanking. For those who like to mix bondage and spanking, there is a whole array of techniques and equipment available, but if you simply want a little more control, then clothes are always useful. Use his tie to fasten his hands behind his back, or her stockings to tie both wrists and ankles, while a jacket can be pulled down at the back to trap the wearer's arms and knickers knotted off around her ankles or knees, or even fixed to a chair leg.

Use his tie to fasten his hands behind his back, or her stockings to tie both wrists and ankles.

Trousers, shirtsleeves, bras, scarves, shoelaces, belts can all be pressed into service; just about anything except footwear, which can always be put to good use as an impromptu implement.

Even the idea of accepting a spanking is enough to set some people blushing, never mind how it feels to be put across the knee or laid bare, but when it comes to erotic humiliation that is only the beginning. Most people who like to be spanked accept a bare bottom as necessary or at least inevitable, but having their legs opened or their cheeks pulled apart is a step further and may even be a hard limit.

> Spanking is all about your bottom, and a lot of people like to include anal play, maybe just being shown off, maybe being tickled, even penetrated.

Spanking is all about your bottom, and a lot of people like to include anal play, maybe just being shown off, maybe being tickled, or even penetrated. Having a plug in your bottom hole while you're being spanked definitely adds a certain something, both to the sensation and to your feelings, especially with the implication of what might happen afterwards. A favourite trick to play with any implement that has a smooth, rounded handle is to complete the spanking ritual by sticking it up your partner's bottom. Then there's figging, which we've already looked at in sensation play but goes perfectly with a good spanking, or, better still, with six of the best.

> Figging: The act of inserting a piece of carved ginger root into your partner's bottom hole before their spanking.

Don't neglect the front end either. A blindfold can add to feelings of uncertainty and trepidation, or a top can be pulled up to cover the head. Or, if things are getting too noisy, you might want to use a gag. This doesn't have to

be anything fancy, just take her knickers off and stuff them in her mouth, as in the next picture of Leia-Ann, which also shows another favourite – even if it is a seasonal one – being made to go out in the snow to cool off your freshly smacked bottom.

Alternatively – and I say alternatively because it's a little difficult with a mouthful of wet cotton – have your partner bent over something rather than OTK and mix in a little oral sex between salvoes of smacks. Or make her hold something in her mouth while she's spanked, perhaps a nice red apple, issuing extra smacks if it falls out.

With a girl, bare her breasts, just because it's so unnecessary.

There's also a lot of power in unnecessary exposure, particularly for a girl if you bare her breasts, which is both exciting and humiliating simply because it's so unnecessary, or strip your partner slowly

With a boy, put him in bra and panties, ideally frilly and pink.

as the spanking proceeds, so that she starts fully dressed, and preferably smartly dressed too, and ends up in the nude. This can work in reverse for a boy, Why not put him in bra and panties, or have him cross-dress completely, as this would play a good part in a complete

164

spanking ritual in any male submissive scenario.

Underwear can also be used for control and
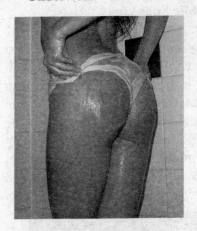 stimulation, pulled up tight between the cheeks and tugged to the same rhythm as the spanking, which can even bring some people to climax. A pair of reasonably full knickers is also ideal for holding in a few cubes of ice, a handful of glutinous mud or perhaps a nice sticky cream cake, but that's moving towards messy fun, which deserves a chapter of its own. Wet skin also stings more, making the perfect excuse for a spanking at bath time, as shown. She has her knickers on in the bath so that she can pull them up and down between smacks to keep her cheeks wet.

There's even more fun to be had with an audience, if that's your thing, but bear in mind that just because a girl likes her knickers stuck in her mouth and a plug up her bottom or a boy likes to be in frilly knickers and bra in the privacy of your bedroom

If the embarrassment of being spanked can be overwhelming, then to be spanked in front of somebody else is something else altogether.

doesn't mean they can cope with the same treatment in front of several hundred kinky club goers. If the embarrassment of being spanked can be overwhelming, then to be spanked in front of somebody else is something else altogether.

Group Spankings and Public Spankings

If involving other people is your thing, then you have a whole new set of pleasures to explore, but make no mistake, giving a spanking in front of people is involving them, so be very sure that they're going to enjoy the experience, just as you would if they were going to be actively involved. You also need to be careful about where you are and who might be watching, although, frankly, so long as there's no bare flesh on display no casual passer-by is likely to make a fuss over a few

smacks, especially if it's a male bottom on the receiving end and a woman dishing it out.

Perhaps the best way to do it is to find another couple with compatible tastes, which ensures an appreciative, understanding audience and allows you to take it one step further and exchange partners, if that's what you want. Now that we have the internet, it's easy to find spanking partners, but I find that most people view spanking as playful fun anyway, just so long as it's under the right circumstances. For some people, there is still a stigma attached, so it's wise to be discreet, but any open minded couple should have no difficulty in finding other people to join in their spanking games, or at very least, a voyeur who understands the rules of the game and what is and is not acceptable.

> Any open-minded couple should have no difficulty in finding other people to join in their spanking games.

Whether you're an exhibitionist, or whether it's the added humiliation of having something so intimate done in front of somebody else, you'll appreciate the extra thrill, and once you're fully into it, and have a group of like-minded friends the possibilities are endless. I've been enjoying small, intimate spanking groups for 25 years and going to bigger clubs for 15, which has given me immense pleasure and all at rather less cost than ordinary parties and nights on the town.

The important thing at spanking parties is to break the ice. We found that the best way to do this was to play games with spanking and other kinky pleasures as forfeits; usually dice or cards, but also custom-made computer games. That way, not only do you get things going, but you get over the often thorny question of who does what with who. We also found that the games work best if the loser who has to pay the forfeit is allowed at least some choice in what happens.

> For a spanking party to work well there can be no room for petty jealousy.

Choosing your guests carefully is also essential. For a spanking party to work well there can be no room for

167

petty jealousy, or for those too shy to take it in front of other people, and everybody has to understand the basic etiquette for the group. One person who expects to join in but won't let anybody else play with his or her partner can ruin the entire evening.

It's not essential that everybody be prepared to switch, because rules can always be adapted accordingly, but my experience is that it's a lot more fun if everybody has to accept a chance of being on the receiving end. That helps to build tension, while reducing people's concerns about allowing others to spank them, because there's always a chance of revenge. Our most successful game, Sweet Revenge, was built around the principle of getting your own back, but we'll come to that at the end of the book.

Guests also have to be balanced. It's easy if you're gay or so easy-going that everybody is happy to play with everybody else, but otherwise you need to make sure that there are more or less equal numbers of men and women, or at least that one half of your guests are prepared to spank or be spanked by the other half.

You can make a game as complicated as you like and adapt it to your own tastes, but it'll work best if you know your guests' favourite fantasies and can work them in, such as being punished by somebody of the same sex or passed around from lap to lap for an OTK session with every single other guest. What is absolutely essential is complete trust in each other's discretion, which is why there's no picture included from a spanking party.

At fetish clubs, you get a bigger audience and it's a great way to draw the attention of like-minded people, but have no control over who's watching, which can lead to problems with those who don't understand the etiquette.

Taking it

> The art of taking a spanking lies in making the pleasure balance the pain.

To enjoy taking a spanking, it's generally necessary to find a balance between pleasure and pain, even when being spanked is your favourite fantasy. There are exceptions. If your pleasure lies in the pain itself, or in anticipation, or knowing you're being punished, or in having been punished, or in some combination of these things, then the pain is an essential part of the fantasy. There's still the question of how much you need, but that's entirely an individual matter, save only that you have a responsibility to look after your welfare, as does whoever is giving the punishment.

Otherwise, it's a question of how much you can cope with in order to let your endorphins build up. For some people, it's easy to 'melt into' the spanking, allowing your natural responses to take over, sometimes all the way to orgasm. Others find it harder and need to treated with enough care and attention or it simply won't work. That takes a patient, considerate top, but people who find the idea of being spanked arousing will be OK as long as they're warmed slowly, however sensitive they are. Anybody can take a pat on the bum, after all, and as your flesh

> For some people, it's easy to 'melt into' the spanking, allowing your natural responses to take over, sometimes all the way to orgasm.

warms, you'll find those pats need to be harder in order to give the same effect, until the pats become smacks, and, before you know it, you'll be taking a full blown spanking. Be careful though, because I've known people to start off wincing at really quite gentle smacks and end up begging for it to be as hard as possible as they come, only to end up needing a cushion to sit down on for the next week.

Once you're used to being spanked, you may prefer your partner to start quite hard, relying on the psychology of the situation to see you through until your endorphins kick in, which will help you over the pain barrier, something you'll soon come to recognise. Not that it's always the same, by any means, because all sorts of things can change the way your body reacts, but if you want it, you'll probably be able to cope.

If you want to take implements, I strongly advise a warm-up spanking first. A single cane stroke given on cold flesh when the receiver isn't in the right head space can be enough to ruin things permanently, even when being given a hard caning is your favourite fantasy. So, unless you're experienced, I suggest spending a while over your partner's knee being spanked and caressed until you feel you're ready. If you're the one dishing it out, be patient and learn to read your partner's body. There's no way to lose a playmate faster than to go in too hard too soon.

> Afterglow – The warm, happy feeling that comes only after a good spanking.

Aftercare

A spanking can also be an extraordinarily intense experience. If you've been on the receiving end, you'll be feeling all sorts of emotions; arousal, excitement, joy, gratitude or maybe resentment, contrition, defiance, in addition to a warm, happy glow that you can't get any other way. You may want sex then and there, or to cuddle the person who's just spanked you, no longer caring for your exposure as long as you can melt into them. Spanking can be wonderfully cathartic, or it can leave you feeling completely helpless in your lover's arms. Being stroked and kissed as you're gently coaxed towards sex is bliss, and the sense of absolute surrender that comes with penetration after a good spanking is a joy all its own, a unique experience that nobody who hasn't done it can even begin to understand. Or you may just want revenge.

> The sense of absolute surrender that comes with penetration after a good spanking is a joy all its own.

If you've been dishing it out, bear in mind that partners may be feeling vulnerable and need affirmation of your feelings, so a cuddle can be very important. If they want to hold onto you, even to cry, cling on tight and put your own needs to the side until they're ready. Make sure they know you love and respect them, not in spite of what they've done, but because of what they've done.

Once you're sure your partner is OK, then there's all sorts of fun to be had. Anybody who's been spanked should always say thank you, at very least with a kiss both for you and any implement that's been used on the bottom, but you might think oral sex given with your partner kneeling at your feet a more appropriate reward. Or you might like to kiss him or her better, on all four cheeks, while, if you're calm, cool and collected, it can be fun to make your

> Anybody who's been spanked should always say thank you.

partner do corner time, which is a whole other ritual.

Traditionally, whoever has been spanked should stand in the corner with bare red bottom showing to the room and hands on head. A wall does equally well, perhaps with the nose touching it and a book balanced on the head. Outdoors, a tree works just as well, and with a girl, it's a nice touch to have her hold her top up in place of

putting her hands on her head. Whatever you choose to do, the idea is for your partner to contemplate his or her sins while you enjoy the view and perhaps a quiet drink, but, as the picture shows, it doesn't always work that way.

Last of all, it's kind to rub soothing cream into smacked cheeks, which is best done with your partner in the ever-popular OTK position and it might well kick things off again.

Coming Out?

For most people, sex is something you do in private, however kinky it may get, and which you keep to yourselves. If you do like to be more open, whether it's just meeting like-minded people, playing at clubs or going the whole hog and playing with other people, there couldn't be a better time than now or a better place than the UK. There may have been fetish clubs in the 70s and before, but they were small, private and firmly underground. In 1983, Club Maîtresse opened in London's Soho, closely followed by Der Putsch. Ten years later, London alone had five regular fetish clubs, and with the success of the SM Pride protest movement and the arrival of the internet things took off exponentially. Most British cities now have at least one club, and regular munches are held even in small towns.

Munches are the place to start; small, informal, with no dress code, which allows you to get to know like-minded people and decided if you'd like to go on to a full scale club. They are generally held in pubs and are open to anybody who's interested. It is easier if you're in a couple, and social skills are as important in the fetish scene as anywhere else, but my own experience is that most people are friendly and welcoming, while there is a wonderful sense of belonging that comes from being with people who understand you and who you can talk to openly about your sexuality.

The next step is going to a club, which can be quite daunting the first time, so it might be an idea to arrange to go in a group with friends you've made at munches. To get on at clubs, you do need to be aware of basic etiquette, but it's really no more than good manners and common sense. First and foremost, never touch without being invited. It's perfectly OK to watch whatever is going on, but leave people a reasonable amount of personal space, especially if they're wielding an implement. It's not acceptable to push in, or to disturb people in the heat of the moment, but if you're playing, or have been playing, don't be offended if other people ask if they can join in. You have every right to refuse, but if you're giving a show in front of other people, you can hardly complain if they're interested. Be tolerant of other people's kinks, just as you'd like them to be tolerant of yours. Cameras are usually banned outright, but if there is an official photographer, he or she should ask you permission before including you in a shot. Do try and dress the part, because otherwise you might well not get through the door and because people will react better if you've made an effort. Lastly, remember that everybody there is an individual human being, just like you. Treat them that way and you'll get along fine.

Messy
Fun

Rude Food and the Joy of
Splosh

Messy fun is where sex meets slapstick and playing with your food takes on a whole new meaning. Most kinky sex needs explaining in terms of deep, sometimes dark, needs and intense feelings that aren't easily understood unless you've experienced them, but this is pure, playful, childish fun. It doesn't even have that much to do with power exchange, as the usual rule is

> Push a custard pie in his face and he's likely to drop one down your knickers.

that if you push a custard pie in my face I'm going to do my best to push one in yours.?????. What it does rely on is that fine borderline between disgust and delight, on laughter, on mischief and on revenge but above all, on playfulness.

That's the key, even more so than with spanking, because while messy fun can be as rude, as humiliating and as arousing as anything else, it's seldom painful. It is messy though, by definition, and that does mean it's a rather specialist taste. Plenty of people are into messy fun but nothing else kinky, while plenty of otherwise very kinky people don't like it at all. Others enjoy some aspects but not all, and there's certainly a wide range, from really rather elegant and civilised food play to full on, no holds barred mud wrestling. That variety is reflected in what people get out of it, from very subtle, delicate pleasures of sight and taste to a heady jumble of sensations; glutinous, slippery and filthy all at once and maybe vulnerable and embarrassing into the bargain.

> Start off in immaculate evening wear and end up naked and slippery on a pile of soggy clothing.

In common with so many sexy things, taboo breaking is part of the fun, even if it's just being messy for the hell

of it after a lifetime of being told to wash your hands and face, mind your table manners and not get covered in paint, mud or chocolate cake. That's why for most people who are into messy fun, contrast is crucial. Playing naked in a mess of bananas and custard is great, but to start off in immaculate evening wear and end up naked and slippery as you have sex on a pile of soggy clothing can be even better.

Still, unless you don't mind spending more time cleaning up than you do playing, it's best to follow a few basic ground rules. For a start, it's generally a good idea to use a splash mat. DIY stores stock plastic sheeting designed to protect carpets and furniture when decorating, which work well for all but the messiest play, although I did once come down in the morning after a fine party to discover taramasalata on the ceiling. If you're going to wrestle, or wear stiletto heels, you might be better off with a heavy-duty pond liner.

The sensible place to play is the bathroom, especially if it's fully tiled, but for some people that feels like cheating, and doubly so if you go in the shower or tub, precisely because it is sensible. Naughty is always fun. If you are fortunate enough to have a garden that's not overlooked, a paddling pool is ideal, or if you're on the right kind of soil, you can make a mud wallow with a few minutes spadework and a garden hose.

> You might feel that playing where it's easy to clean up spoils the fun.

Outdoors, you need to watch out for sharp stones and

twigs in mud, while a good tolerance of creepy crawlies can be a big help. Lonely beaches and lakes are often good sites, but when a country walk is likely to end up with both of you covered in mud it's a good idea to keep water, towels, plastic sheeting and long coats in the car.

Whatever you play with, especially paint, make sure it's water soluble, non-toxic and easily cleaned.

> Would you choose a spanking, or a can of baked beans poured over your head?

Messy fun is also perfect for kinky games, whether it's a punishment, a forfeit, or perhaps best of all, a competition, in which one of you is going to get it but it all depends on the turn of a card or the fall of a set of dice. This works especially well if you're playing in a group, as there are plenty of people who are lots of fun but aren't into pain and so appreciate a choice between, for example, taking a spanking and having a few tomatoes dropped down their pants.

Food

I imagine everybody has enjoyed a bit of food play, maybe feeding each other strawberries mouth to mouth or sucking honey from your lover's fingers. Taking it a little further, the natural plate for sexy food is a girl's chest; picturesque, sensitive and just crying out for artistic creativity.

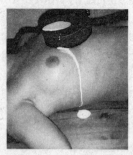

Try it as a birthday treat, carefully timed and arranged so that he comes in to find the table fully laid; china, crystal, candles, flowers and you, laid naked on the table with an exquisitely prepared meal set out with you as the plate, from the smoked salmon canapé ready to be nibbled from your lips to the *pièce de résistance*, a strategically placed chocolate mousse. You might want to choose aphrodisiacs for every course; perhaps starting with avocado and ginger in your mouth, oysters on your breasts, then steak with asparagus in a mustard sauce as the main course before moving on to the chocolate mousse. For the true gourmet, you could even set out a selection of appropriate wines.

> Cold food can do nipples the world of good, chocolate melts into every crevice and spices make the skin tingle and sting.

(Note to partners: be sure to share as you go along, and make sure you lick up the mousse properly to say thank you.)

If that's a little elaborate, *hors d'oeuvres* or a sweet treat make perfect toppings for your breasts or the cheeks of your bottom, while an ice cream can be just the thing for spanking aftercare. Cold things can do nipples the world of good too, chocolate will melt into every crevice, while spicy food tingles and stings the skin. Hot food is better still, although you need to test the temperature very carefully before serving. The picture shows two individual chocolate puddings served piping hot on the cheeks of Sarah's bottom.

Preparation is mostly common sense – such as cutting the steak into bite sized pieces before arranging them on your tummy and

not serving anything too hot – but it will take time and patience, as good food always does. Oh, and far be it from me to criticise anybody's personal taste, but it's probably a good idea to depilate first, especially for gentlemen.

You probably wouldn't want to read the story about my friend and the Christmas turkey.

Not that you have to eat the food you play with, of course. The possibilities offered by a courgette don't need explaining, and you probably wouldn't want to read the story about my friend and the Christmas turkey, but food is inherently messy and it's a lot harder to think of anything you can't have fun with than the other way around. What you do need is a sense of fun, and either to take pleasure in messy, sticky, slippery sensations for their own sake or enjoy the feelings of humiliation they can bring.

For most people, this sort of food play is more fun with clothes than without, just because it's messier, and that doesn't mean it's any less rude. Underwear is ideal for holding mess in and against the most intimate parts of your body. The photo shows a girl who has had half-a-dozen large, free-range eggs put down her panties, which are being broken one at a time by her friend. I'm sure you can imagine how she felt as the mess got gradually worse until the contents of her panties were running down her thighs and soaking slowly over her bottom and between

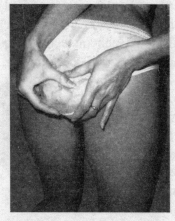

her legs. Her only complaint was that the broken shells were a bit scratchy, which is just the sort of minor problem you're likely to encounter.

It's usually best to avoid hard things, although in this case it was all part of the fun. There's a strong yuk factor to messy food, and eggs definitely have it, raw or cooked, as does anything else slimy, slippery or sticky, also anything that can be inserted in a convenient orifice.

The Yuk Factor
A Menu
Smooth Goose Liver and
Orange Paté
*

Bangers and Mash with
Baked Beans and Mushy Peas
*

Steamed Marmalade Pudding
with Custard
*

Cream Cheese

The more intimate and embarrassing the situation the better, by and large, but the acme of food play comes with making a mess in somebody's face. Perhaps it's not as openly sexual, but in many ways, your face is you, and to have it pushed into something wet and squishy is not to be taken casually, even if the wet and squishy thing is a delicious chocolate cake. Having it done in your face also gives you the best possible opportunity for apprehension if you know it's coming, and for shock if you don't. Your face is where your senses are concentrated, so you do not only feel that cake, but you see it coming, and then smell it and taste it when it hits.

Mud

Fans of mud will point out that, unlike food, there's an effectively infinite supply of the stuff and it's free. That's true, and if you can't eat it, that's not the end of the world, but playing in mud is definitely one for the warmer months. Even then, it's a good idea to search for good sites before you use them, and to plan the event carefully.

> If you want to go mud wallowing, plan the event carefully.

There's nothing illegal about getting covered in mud, and being dressed is often part of the fun anyway, while, if you do get caught, you can always say you fell in. Nevertheless, most people prefer a bit of privacy, while you also need to find somewhere with the right sort of

mud. The main problem is that mud is all too often full of other things. Muddy estuaries where there is oyster farming are about the worst case I've heard of, because the mud looks appealing but is full of bits of razor sharp shell. Farmland can be equally tempting, as there's often plenty of good, glutinous mud, but if there are animals around, particularly cows, it may be a bit more glutinous than you had bargained for. Stones and twigs can also be a problem, and it's wise to avoid areas where there's a lot of gorse growing. You also need to be aware of the possibilities of pollution, and keep your face clean.

So, choose your mud first. Clay soil is best, as it drains slowly and the small particles make for a nice, slippery consistency, especially if it's been churned up by tractor wheels and allowed to settle. The smaller particles stay at the top, leaving a layer of fine soil. Wet sand can also be good, especially by the sea where the particles are smooth, but coarse sand or gravel is no fun at all unless you want the experience to be painful as well as messy.

For the picture, we found a wonderful wallow deep in the woods on sandy soil overlying heavy clay, so while most of the wood was dry, there were a few pools of thick, sticky mud. The

> Clay soil produces smooth, heavy mud ideal for wallowing in or shovelling down panties.

one Sarah is in was about six inches deep, with a little water lying on top of the mud and no unpleasant bits and pieces.

One great advantage of enjoying mud play is that you love what most people will go out of their way to avoid, so a remote muddy path on a warm, damp day is not only paradise but deserted. Fairly deserted anyway, but if you're going to play with mud in public spaces, you have to accept that you're going to be seen at least occasionally and be ready to adjust your behaviour accordingly.

Having found a site that suits your needs, the next problem is to get there, have your fun and get back. If you just don't care, then good for you, but most people prefer not to attract too much attention. Using a car means you can explore far afield but however many plastic sheets, towels and old coats you bring, the interior is going to get muddy. Off-road bikes are good, both because you can get to places efficiently and because people expect mountain bikers to be covered in mud anyway.

If all of the above sounds like too much hard work, then it is possible to buy mud, which is fine for small quantities, but if you want a really good wallow on a regular basis, it's going to be fairly expensive. Modelling clay is ideal, smooth and slippery, while if you play in the bath or a paddling pool you should be able to retrieve most of it afterwards. It also washes away quite easily, but you do need to be careful not to block the drains. Alternatively, you can buy soil or sand from your local DIY store and mix up your own mud, but it's wise to experiment first, and whatever you do, don't buy cement.

Paint

Like food, there are two different angles to playing with paint, erotic body painting and splosh.

There are several different takes on erotic body painting, from simple pretty patterns, maybe of butterflies or flowers, and often designed to emphasise the contours of your body, through bolder, more openly sexual designs, to

A paint filled balloon makes the perfect messy missile.

the deliciously cheeky fashion for painted-on clothes. Often based around sports kit, models are painted in such a way that, at first glance, you seem to be properly dressed, if in tight clothing, and only on closer inspection does it become obvious that you're actually nude. Most popular of all are football colours, which have bold striking designs that distract the eye from what's really going on. The best thing to use is theatrical body paint, which is designed for the job in hand, water soluble and easy to find.

Splosh with paint may be less artistic, but it's just as much fun. Arts and crafts shop stock big containers of  cheap, non toxic water soluble paint which you can play with safely in much the same way as with a light mud, only far more colourful and easier to wash away. It's ideal for play fights as well, either as it comes or squeezed into balloons to make the perfect messy missile, although paint needs to be diluted a little to work in water pistols. Serious mess is guaranteed, so paint fighting is definitely one for the garden, but hosing each other down afterwards can be as much fun as the main event.

Even with non-toxic, water soluble paint you'll want to keep it out of your eyes, so goggles might be a good idea, and never play with paints that use anything other than water as a solvent.

Messy Punishments

Messy fun can also add an extra something to power exchange games. Food and mud are excellent for giving humiliating punishments,

Boot blacking is just the thing for a naughty bottom.

especially for recreating real ones as play. Perhaps better still is boot polish, as anybody who's had his or her bottom blacked will agree, although when done for real it

was more often as a cruel joke than a punishment.

Then there's messy spanking, because a handful of something squishy down the panties gives taking a smacked bottom a whole new dimension. In the picture – kindly donated by the doyen of all things messy, Bill Shipton – things have gone a little further, because while the girl being spanked has clearly had the worst of it, both of them are fairly liberally plastered with chocolate mousse. So even if you're on top, don't expect to keep your dignity intact. They also appear to have been playing with a pillory, an upright frame with holes for the hands and feet, and once a feature of every village green, where offenders could be locked for public display and revenge, including being pelted with food, generally rotten food. Stocks are similar, but with the board set lower so that the offender stays in a kneeling or sitting position instead of standing and bent forward.

Take a pillory, some semolina pudding, a pound of ripe tomatoes, a couple of black bananas and the possibilities are endless.

A pillory is a great way to combine messy fun with bondage, spanking and sex as well. Choose your food carefully though. Rotten eggs may be traditional, but they're too hard if you're doing it for fun. Go for something soft and squashy, like over-ripe tomatoes or balls made of dough and filled with raw egg. It seems only fair to throw your missiles, and he may find it worse not knowing if you're going to hit or miss, but you may prefer to be a bit more hands on, in which case you don't have to worry about aerodynamics and can use spray cream, mushy peas, black bananas, a bowl of blancmange maybe, or a jug of custard. The possibilities are endless.

> First show them the treacle and feathers, so they can savour what is about to happen.

Another kinky version of an old-fashioned punishment is a playful but still extremely messy version of tarring and feathering. Real tar is out of the question because it needs to be hot and can damage your skin as well, but black treacle makes a perfect substitute, while an old pillow provides a ready source of small feathers. I recommend doing it slowly, with your playmate first stripped, then tied to a small tree with their hands behind the trunk. Two or three big cans of treacle should be enough, first shown to him or her so what is about to happen can be savoured, then poured slowly over the head so that it trickles down the body and can be rubbed in by hand. Tip some of the feathers over your partner and throw the rest from close range to make sure he or she gets an even covering, after which it might be kind to relieve what ought to be some serious sexual tension, but not until you've taken a few photos for the album.

Food Fights & Messy Wrestling

In my experience, any messy fun involving food is more likely to end in a food fight than not. In fact, this next picture – which is not posed –shows what was a perfectly civilised birthday treat of sherry trifle served on a girl's chest until Peter's wife decided he was being greedy and

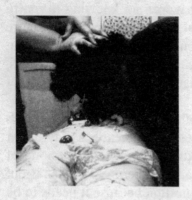

pushed his face into the half-eaten mess. We never did manage to get all the stains off the furniture, and that's the drawback of food fights – the aftermath. Otherwise, they're not only great fun but can be just as sexy as you like to make them.

Domestic accidents are a hazard, and there is also a serious risk to your dignity. At one particularly glorious school dinner cabaret, we served bangers and mash with mushy peas, an ideal combination except that the floor rapidly became too slippery to stand up at all easily, while three of the girls ganged up on the unfortunate "master", sat on him and stuck a sausage up his bottom.

The same set-up in a ring would have been messy wrestling, which is the one aspect of messy fun that has become mainstream, if hardly respectable, but in common with most mainstream kinky erotica, it's mainly

> Three of the girls ganged up on the unfortunate master

to do with women wrestling in gooey substances for the entertainment of male watchers. That's fine by me, but in practices, you're much more likely to be wrestling with your partner, of whatever sex. If so, you probably don't have a professional ring and gallons of play mud, but a paddling pool will do just as well, preferable on some soft surface, like long grass.

Whatever you choose to wrestle in, bear in mind that it's going to get everywhere, and I do mean everywhere. Play mud is okay, but not garden mud, while if you're going to use food you need something that can be bought quite cheaply in bulk, unless of course you feel you can afford to wrestle in caviar or *foie gras*, in which case good luck to you. For ordinary mortals, catering sized tins are more practical and contain some seriously high yuk factor foods; baked beans, spaghetti hoops, chilli con carne perhaps, or if you want to be really disgusting, several different ones mixed in together, perhaps with some of those little slippery sausages included.

Many cheap, high yuk factor foods come in catering sized tins.

After all, the aim is usually not only to beat partners but to playfully humiliate them too, at the very least by getting them as messy as possible, especially down their clothes and in the face, maybe by stripping them as well and very possibly ending with sex in the position of the victor's choice. Oh, and keep a hose handy so that, if necessary, you can start to wash down without having to open your eyes first.

You aim is less to win than to humiliate your opponent.

Clowning

Clowning is a rare and specialised form of erotic play that doesn't have to be messy but usually is, although it's definitely one for the dedicated enthusiast. A costume can be made up from bits and pieces to excellent effect, but, even then, you need to get the make-up right and that takes practice. Others prefer a full-on clown costume, which can come quite expensive, even if you make it yourself. As always with clothing for sex, some will feel the need for the authentic look, sometimes good enough for them to be able to walk into any big top in the land and have no questions asked.

Others prefer an eroticised version and would be arrested on the spot as these are typically skin tight and leave all the rudest bits showing. Either way, you're going to look ridiculous, but that's the whole idea. Sarah's outfit in the picture is simple but effective; size 10 boots on tiny feet, red knee socks, frilly pink panties, red and white ribbons for her hair with a white face, blue eye liner and bright red lipstick for her mouth, cheeks, nose and nipples. Quite what she's planning to do with the giant spanking paddle and the extra large sausage roll with Scotch eggs, I shall leave to your imagination.

You're sure to look ridiculous, but that's the idea.

Once you get down to it, messy clowning is really a different take on erotic competition, but one in which cunning counts for as much as strength and agility. Custard pies are the weapons of choice, and the aim is to splosh your partner as thoroughly as possible while avoiding getting sploshed yourself, probably while trying to strip and spank each other at the same time. You need plenty of space, and a splash mat.

Multiple Partners

For the great majority of people, sex, and all things sexual, involves two people. Most people who enjoy kinky sex are the same, but less conventional relationships are quite common. This can happen for a number of reasons. You may simply have a casual attitude to monogamy and enjoy multiple partners, either singly or together. If that's the case, good luck to you, be safe and have fun.

Alternatively, it may be that one or other partner cannot fully express their sexuality within their relationship, if they're bisexual for instance, although it doesn't necessarily follow that if you're bisexual you can't be perfectly happy in a monogamous relationship. I know of many examples of relationships in which one partner has a strong need for something the other cannot give, for whatever reason, and because of the taboo nature of many of the practices I've covered in this book, it's extremely easy to get deep into a relationship before you discover this fact.

A typical example would be a man who feels the need to be dominated sexually but has a partner who finds the idea unacceptable, embarrassing or perhaps wants to be dominated herself. Even if she's perfectly willing to try, it may be that without a streak of natural sexual dominance he remains unsatisfied. If that's the case, you can either put up with it, go behind your partner's back or come to an agreement. The first two options are clearly unsatisfying, although sadly they are the ones most often taken. Reaching an agreement isn't easy either, but it can work. No two agreements will ever be exactly the same, so it is impossible to give specific advice, only a few pointers, which also apply to open relationships.

* Set your limits and stick to them. If you've agreed that spanking is OK, spank away to your heart's content but don't let it go any further.
* Only play with people who understand how your arrangement works and respect your limits, both emotionally and physically.
* Beware of sexual predators, the emotionally needy and anybody whose aim is to break up your relationship. It's often better to play with couples.
* What's good for the goose is good for the gander. If you want freedom but won't give it to your partner, you are courting disaster.
* If you can, play together as a threesome, foursome etc. That way, the experience can make your relationship stronger, but always put your partner first.
* Don't compare your partner unfavourably with other people, either physically or in terms of what they can and cannot do.

Having said all that, it would be wrong to deny that allowing other people to be involved in your relationship doesn't pose a risk. In my experience, complicated, multi-partner relationships generally don't last as long as conventional ones, but that doesn't mean they never work. The same is true for very intense kinky relationships, even when both partners are perfectly compatible. In both instances, it's usually a case of the brighter the flame the quicker it dies, but my partner and I celebrated our 25th anniversary last year, looking back happily at all the playmates we've shared.

Altered

Nature

Ponies and Puppies and Things
that go Oink in the Woods

Before I go any further I want to make one thing absolutely clear. This chapter has nothing to do with bestiality. Nothing whatsoever. OK? There's no need to ring the RSPCA. OK? There's no need to get on your high horse. (Sorry, I couldn't resist that one.)

What it's about is the desire to take on the characteristics of another animal. You only have to look at the gods of the ancient Egyptians and the Hindus, the Greek myths, American Indian cultures or old European legend to see that this is something deeply ingrained in the human psyche. It's by no means always related to erotica, but this is a practical guide to kinky play, so I'll focus on what's popular and what's sexy. Not that everybody finds the idea of taking on animal characteristics sexy, by any means, and I appreciate that the idea leaves a lot of people bemused. If that's you, bear with me and maybe I can change your mind.

> Ancient cultures show the desire of humans to take on the aspect of another animal.

Let's start with the commonest image, which is in fact, so well known it's a bit cheesy – the bunny-girl. Unfortunately, the Playboy bunny-girl has had a bit of a mixed press due to being linked with mainstream commercial erotica, and especially men's clubs, which gives the impression that it's all about girls dressing up in cute costumes for the satisfaction of men. I'm not saying it's wrong to do that, but it's not what I want to explore. What I do want to explore is how both men and women choose to express themselves as animals, not for other people's pleasure, and certainly not for money, but

> It's not all about girls dressing up in cute costumes for the satisfaction of men.

for their own satisfaction. Besides, Hugh Heffner's bunny-girls have cute fluffy tails and big ears, but I always felt they should have prominent front teeth and wrinkly noses as well.

I always felt Hugh Heffner's bunny-girls should have prominent front teeth and wrinkly noses as well as cute fluffy tails and big ears.

After all, if you're going to do something, why not do it in style?

Some people do, but the bunny-girl is a creature more often created for the sake of fancy dress than outright kink. Cat-girl imagery is also quite popular in the mainstream, and has a better image, but is also a favourite in kinky circles, although the two most popular choices are puppies, of both sexes, and the most elaborate of all, ponies.

Whatever your choice, the essence of the fantasy is to take on whatever characteristics of that animal you find appealing, both in imagery and behaviour. For some, it is

simply an excuse to look cute, or a chance to shed human

responsibilities and inhibitions, while others wish to identify with their choice as fully as possible, developing a full animal *alter-ego*. Most people like to choose a pet name, or to be named, so that for this chapter, Leia-Ann becomes Queenie pony-girl and Sophie become Candi the kitten.

For myself, it is light-hearted, sexy fun, and not only for its own sake, but because it combines elements of domination and submission, erotic display, bondage, spanking and messy fun. Bring all that together and you have what is not only a delightful kink, but the most clubbable of all. You can hold shows and competitions, run races and hunts, play all sorts of games, all of which is, quite simply, immense fun.

A kink that combines elements of domination and submission, erotic display, bondage, spanking and messy fun.

Then there's the wonderful elaboration of the fantasy, which for me is a pleasure in itself. Every aspect of animal behaviour and of human interaction with that animal can be translated into erotic play, which I and others have used to create a world of fantastic complexity and eroticism, as you will see.

Taking on an animal role is nearly always a submissive fantasy; whether your desire is to be treated like a pet, like a beast of burden, to be tamed, or to be chased and caught. There are a few exceptions, both where it is the dominant partner who takes on the animal role and for which both partners do so, but, by and large, the fantasy is focussed on the submissive partner, with the dominant partner in a compatible human role; owner to a pony-boy, master to a

To appreciate these fantasies needs a flexible and vivid imagination.

puppy-girl, or whatever it might be.

Whatever role you take, these fantasies require a flexible and vivid imagination to appreciate, although I've always been pleasantly surprised how many people come new to the idea and take it up with enthusiasm. Others have the need within themselves and feel driven to express it, often leading to creations of fantastic depth and complexity, perhaps more so than for any other kink.

Some roles, such as kitten-play and puppy-play are easy to explore with your partner at home, as you don't really need specialist equipment and, if you do want a costume, they can be purchased quite easily or run up on a sewing machine. More elaborate fantasies need more equipment and more space, pony play especially, and so you might prefer to join a group, some of which are listed in the credits at the end of the book. Shows and hunts only really work if there are quite a few people involved. Exhibitionism is often an important part of the fantasy, but however much people like to show off, they generally prefer an appreciative, understanding audience, which is another good reason for working with like-minded enthusiasts. If you do choose to go down that route, make sure that the balance of people involved suits your own needs and those of your partner.

> Elaborate fantasies need equipment and space, so you might want to join a group.

> Bear in mind legal restrictions on nudity and be careful not to horrify the natives.

Choosing a suitable site can be difficult. Large indoor venues tend to be expensive, while, unless you are fortunate enough to own a country estate, playing outdoors can be a problem, although some groups now own private land for play, another advantage of joining.

Pony play

Pony play is probably the most popular form of animal transformation fantasy and certainly the most fully developed. It's still very rare in comparison with, say, bondage or spanking, but those who do go in for it often put their heart and soul into expressing their fantasy, so much so that the UK alone has several small but dedicated clubs.

Those involved are both sexes and come from all walks of life , but the archetypal pony-girl is a woman who's taken her love of horses so far that she wants to be one, either as closely as possible, or taking on those horsey characteristics that appeal to her erotic sensibilities. She may want to be ridden, harnessed, groomed, trained, guided with a whip, shown in competition, put to work pulling a cart or ploughing a field, even taken to market. To fulfil these needs takes time, effort and expense, yet masters and mistresses are generally in good supply. Pony-boys usually find they need to offer more than simply themselves, perhaps their own gear or a good location.

Once pony play has become part of your relationship, or you've found yourself a playmate or a suitable group, you will almost certainly find yourself wanting equipment. Not that it's absolutely necessary, because a long piece of twine and a switch cut from the hedge will do at a pinch, but, for most people, tack is part of the fun.

The pictures of Palomina and Queenie in this section show harnesses being worn, but it is difficult to make out the details, so I have included a separate plate of a full harness set laid out, exactly as worn by Queenie in the inset picture. It may seem complicated, but it is designed for a club and therefore needs to fit people of all shapes and sizes, rather than being custom made for a partner. There are almost as many designs as there are people into pony play, but the only essentials are a system of bit and reins to allow the pony to be guided. Body harnesses are not strictly necessary unless you are planning to have your pony pull something, in which case it is important to let them take the weight on their shoulders and hips rather than their arms.

Pony harnesses are mainly for show but can also be practical.

In the first picture, you can also see Palomina's tail, which was custom made to match her hair.

Queenie's picture shows her tail more clearly, both in place and on its own to show the stiff rubber spine that leads down between her cheeks and the tail plug, which fits up her bottom. The plug and spine hold her tail in such a way that

it appears to project from the base of her spine in the same way as the tail of a real horse, although it's best to attach the ribbons to the rear of the harness to keep the tail in place during play. Most pony tails have the hair sticking straight out of the plug, leaving it dangling down in an unsightly fashion rather than sticking up at a jaunty angle. Use a condom with plug-in tails, and plenty of lubricant. It's also possible to get stick on tails and tails that attach by a belt or to the harness, which can look good but aren't nearly as much fun.

Several bondage gear makers also produce pony-girl tack, and it's possible to buy just about anything you could possibly need; harness, straps, leads, mittens, even saddles and hoof boots, while accessories include blinkers, headdresses, cheek bells and suitable body jewellery. The only problems are the expense and that your choice of colour is almost certainly going to be black, black or black. You may feel that brown leather is more authentic, enjoy a splash of colour or own a pony-girl with an obsession for pink or lilac. If so, you're either going to have to order your tack custom made by a specialist, and that can come very expensive, or to make your own gear. The set shown can be assembled for around £50.

> It's possible to buy just about anything you could possibly need, so long as it's in black leather.

1 – Body Harness, main section. The rear part of the belt and two padded shoulder straps joined by brass rings. The corseting between the two sections allows the belt to be tightened once it is on

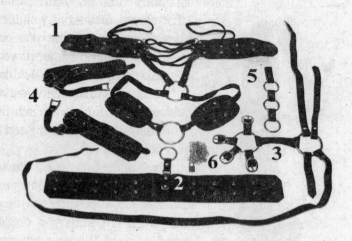

2 – Body Harness, front section. The pins fit into the eyelets on the rear part of the belt, allowing it to be adjusted for waists of between 20"and 60"

3 – Bridle. Two brass rings joined by the bit, which is a roll of soft leather, glued rather than riveted. Metal bits are not suitable for pony-girls. The straps are then joined to the buckles to form the headstall and reins. Working clockwise from the bit, the straps are: head strap, neck strap, reins and chin strap.

4 – Wrist cuffs. Each has an adjustable strap designed to lead to eyes at the end of the shafts or swingletrees.

6 – Ring Strap. A short strap that attaches to the head strap, in this case designed to hold a triple pony-tail. Each

pony tail is then bound with ribbon.

7 – Padlock and Chain. Used to fix the body harness rings together at the centre of the chest, also to link to shafts or a swingletree.

My own feeling is that most commercial pony-girl tack is too obviously a spin-off from ordinary bondage equipment and that you get much better results if you make your own. I like textured leather and heavy brass fittings, matching equipment and, most importantly, to do things my own way. All you need is one good supplier of fittings and another for hides, along with the same leather-working tools as for bondage, although you do need a reasonable level of craft skill and will definitely gain by experience. If you prefer not to use leather, PVC or rubber will do at a pinch, even webbing, but, for me, these are poor substitutes. There are some things you probably won't be able to make, such as the beautiful hoof boots in the picture, which take a great deal of skill.

A visit to a saddlers is also a good idea, because while most of the tack made for real horses is no use at all for human ponies it is possible to get pretty accessories such as rosettes and ribbons, also riding whips at much less than you would pay in a fetish shop.

Having got kitted out as human ponies, they'll probably know what they want to do, and that's likely to include being deeply in role, not talking but communicating by neighs and stamping their hooves, responding to the bit and the whip as much as to verbal commands, and quite possibly being contrary. If they're new to the game, they'll need to be trained, both for the fun of it and because if you're going to attend a show they'll need to be good.

The picture shows Queenie being trained. Basic obedience should come first, learning to respond to the reins and touches of the whip so that she can kneel and stand, move off and halt, turn and back, perhaps first with verbal commands and then without. I've found that stick-and-carrot is the best way to make sure she learns quickly, allowing her to nuzzle a mint from your hand if she does well and putting your whip across her bottom if she doesn't. For training, the best implement is a dressage whip, longer and thinner than an ordinary riding whip with a thin sting ideal for gentle command and firmer reprimand.

Once she has learnt the basic commands, you can teach her different gaits, which are tricky to master but very showy. I found this works best with the pony on a lunge rein, a long rope attached to her harness, or, as shown in the pictures, a swingletree, which is a bar fastened to the front of her harness, which can also be used for carriage driving or pulling a plough. This arrangement allows her to move around you in a circle, just far enough away for the tip of the dressage crop to reach her bottom. When at rest, her feet should be together, her legs and back straight, her head up. For the slowest gait, the walk, she should move forward with short, precise steps, keeping her legs straight at all times. Next is the trot, for which she should bring each knee up in turn so that with each pace her thighs are briefly parallel to the ground. The canter, faster still, is a striding, loping run, while a gallop is a fast run. When training her to gaits, leave her hands free, as this is essential for her sense of balance and in case she should trip.

With her gaits mastered, you might want to move on to jumping, and to full dressage, which requires exact control with whip and rein. Work on a routine, maintaining a regime of reward and punishment until she has mastered it to perfection, by which time she will be ready to compete, if that's the road you want to go down. Even if you don't, by that point she will have been growing more used to her role as your pony-girl with every step of training, which hopefully will allow her to attain a blissfully detached state comparable with skilled bondage or the aftermath of a good spanking.

> It's possible for a human pony to attain a blissfully detached state comparable with skilled bondage or the aftermath of a good spanking.

Some human ponies prefer to be ridden, usually on all fours as shown at the start of the chapter, and in the next picture, which shows the riding position more clearly. For riding to work at all well, the rider needs to be much the lighter of the two, which means that it's more often a game for pony-boys and their mistresses. There are two sorts of saddle generally available. One is designed go on

the back for a crawling pony-boy, as shown, the other to fit onto the hips for a standing pony-boy. Both have stirrups and a girth strap, but the second design needs a wooden frame to sit on and is much harder to make. Pony-carting, in which the human pony is usually harnessed to a single seat buggy or "sulky", is a good alternative to riding but requires some serious equipment and is dealt with separately.

If you do decide to involve other people in your relationship, even if only as onlookers, you open a whole new set of possibilities. Competition is very much a part of real equestrianism, and the same is true of pony play – competition for the winner's rosette can be just as fierce. Individual events will vary and, because of the need for space and privacy, the overheads are quite high, but it's great to mix with like-minded people and to have all the hard work you've put in properly appreciated.

Events may include turnout, for which your pony will be judged on beauty as well as the quality and

presentation of her harness, and also obedience, dressage, jumping, and races, all of which come down to training. It's complicated, obsessive and takes a good deal of time and money, but a good day can leave you with an erotic high like few others.

Pony-carting

The first step is to get a cart. Ordinary pony-carts are designed for horses and therefore too large and too heavy, although I have known a cart originally designed for Shetland ponies put to good use. With two-wheelers there is also the danger of the cart  tipping backwards or the pony losing control on a hill. If you make the cart yourself, it can be designed to suit the human frame, and to work effectively even when the passenger is heavier than the pony. It also needs to be sturdy, capable of taking at least twice the weight of a

Sulky: Any single seat cart, so called because you sit on your own.

heavy rider, and fairly low to the ground or there is a risk of tipping over. You may well want to drive indoors, in which case it should be no wider than a typical doorway.

Even a custom-built sulky has to be big enough to sit

in, which can make it cumbersome and difficult to transport, so if you intend to travel, I advise getting a van or building something that can easily be taken to pieces and reassembled. At the very least, it should be possible to remove the shafts, but ideally you should be able to

disassemble it completely and fit the parts into a car.

My own cart, shown in the pictures, can be assembled both as a sulky, a two-seater and a three-seater carriage, depending on which parts are used. When set up as a sulky, it can be stowed in the boot of all but the very smallest cars and even the carriage parts fit into a small estate. It is also very strong. The main construction is ¾" marine plywood and the parts are joined with M8 bolts, while the seat is placed so as to position the driver's centre of gravity directly above the mid-point of the wheels, which is vital, allowing even a small pony-girl to pull over twice her weight without difficulty on the flat. Built in 1993, it has proved remarkably durable over the years.

Many other designs exist, some for racing, others for

show, but a sulky is basically a seat on wheels and the principles remain the same. The next set of pictures were taken at a race meeting in the English Midlands and show three lightweight sulkies of similar, and typical, design. All are of welded metal construction, but show the same basic combination, of seat, wheels, frame and shafts.

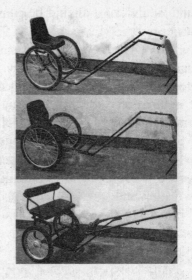

If you choose to buy a ready-made cart or commission one, make sure you test it thoroughly before parting with any cash, or at the very least, assure yourself that it's a tried–and-tested design. Any faults should quickly become apparent, especially if you take it over even moderately rough ground, or it may simply be that the dimensions don't suit you or your partner, especially if you're not an average size.

Cart harnesses should be designed so that you take the weight on your shoulders and hips, not your arms.

A pony-cart needs traces – either ropes or a system of leather straps with which to harness your pony. Ideally this should mean that they are supporting and pulling the cart from the shoulders and hips rather than with the arms, although if the cart is properly balanced, it should move forward quite easily in any case. If you use rope, you are creating what is, in effect, a specialist bondage system, and as always it should be possible to unfasten it quickly if necessary.

Once you've got your cart and all the accessories you can go for a spin. A lot of what you can do is going to depend on your size, for both of you. Inevitably, the best combination for speed and endurance will be a small Mistress and a big, strong pony-boy, but don't let that put you off, even if you're a sumo wrestler and she's a ballerina. With a well designed cart and on the flat you can still have plenty of fun.

An experienced pony should be able to pull a cart with only a little more training. The reins, whip and verbal commands are used to steer and change speed, but there is no standard system and you can add as many refinements as you please. The picture shows Palomina kneeling to allow her driver to dismount. Reversing can be tricky, but as always half the fun is in training and practice anyway.

A small pony-cart can be used at home, but it's far better suited to the great outdoors. Unless you're lucky enough to have private land, this is sure to limit what you can do, but while nudity is unacceptable, there's no law against rickshaws and the worst that's likely to happen is that you get stopped and asked to produce a licence. If this does happen, simply point out that the cart is not for hire. If it is for hire, apply for a licence from the council in the normal way.

Seriously though, space is always a problem for pony-carting enthusiasts and the best solution is to work together, sharing the costs. A flat piece of woodland with a metalled track is ideal, as the carts will run smoothly but can't be seen. If you hire a venue, make sure you have exclusive access, because unless you're very bold indeed, it can be off-putting to have to share your space with motocross riders, mountain bikers and other groups who like to use similar venues.

Being in a group also allows you to expand your horizons, perhaps with larger carts or teams of ponies. Carriage driving is to kinky sex what elephant polo is to sport, but to my mind, it's worth the effort as it allows for full expression of the fetish. My three-seater has been driven through central London, drawn by a four-in-hand, as part of a Pride march from Whitehall to Bloomsbury, which was the perfect opportunity to show it off. That was a rare opportunity at the time, but with the internet now allowing enthusiasts to work together, even this most fanciful form of pony-play is becoming easier to indulge.

Zebra play

Human ponies sometimes prefer to be wild, which changes the dynamic of the fantasy completely, from training and control to the thrill of the chase.

This also dispenses with the need for harness, except perhaps a headstall and a hank of rope, which means you can use body paint and your pony can be piebald, dappled, or even a zebra. It takes between one and two hours to paint somebody from head to toe in zebra-stripes, but the result is gorgeous.

Use ordinary body paint, applied with a one-inch brush and a middling-sized art brush for the detail work. An animal camouflage pattern is usually designed to break up the lines of the body, but erotic body painting should always enhance those lines, which I think works better for a zebra-girl. This is especially true for her lips and eyes, which should be accentuated rather than concealed, as in the picture of Galatea, while similar but bolder patterns can be used to show off her curves. The paint feels cool as it dries, so expect to feel a bit chilly even on a warm summer's day.

> Erotic body painting should enhance the contours of your body.

The four zebra-girls in the second picture are in body paint and also black and white manes and tails. The three who appear to be naked have black bikinis on, carefully painted into the overall design, which allowed  me to photograph them on their way to the pub after an afternoon's hunting.

The tails are made from black and white pony-tail hair extensions and come in two varieties. Some are made in the same way as the pony tail already described, plugging into their bottoms. Others have a broad, triangular base made of thin latex and painted in zebra stripes. This is glued onto their lower backs with gum arabic, which is a

natural gum used as glue in the theatre. Their manes are alternate stripes of black and white hair built up from a latex base and held in place with clips. Theatrical suppliers and the better fancy dress shops stock body paint and gum arabic, while pony-tail hair extensions are available from specialist hairdressers.

As you can see, a lot of work goes into creating the look, and also into the hunt. On the outing shown in the pictures, we played in a large area of private woodland, with the four zebra-girls and five hunters armed with rope and nets to create a classic hunting fantasy.

Including making and buying the gear, setting everything up and painting the girls, the scene must have taken around 24 hours' work. It was also fairly expensive, but worth every penny, especially split nine ways. The only drawback with this

> Hunting fantasies offer lots of opportunities for play together, or better still in a group. Zebra? Fox? Boar? Wolf? Lion? Each has its own flavour.

fantasy is that body paint is messy stuff. It can take two or

213

three baths to get rid of it properly and travelling is a nightmare. Even more so than for pony play, you get a lot more out of zebra play if you work in a group. It will also help to learn how to work with all the different materials involved, and most importantly, with liquid latex.

Liquid Latex

Working with liquid latex makes it possible to bring many aspects of animal transformation to life. It comes as an opaque white liquid and sets to a flexible and reasonably durable rubber of a transparent tan colour, unless you mix in dye, in which case a few drops will give a permanent, intense colour. Most arts and crafts shops stock it, and also thickener.

Liquid latex can be painted onto smooth, non-absorbent surfaces and peeled off as shaped rubber when dry. It will cling to absorbent surfaces and can also be used as a glue to stick leather and bind hair, which makes it perfect for stick on tails such as those the zebra-girls are wearing, or in the picture of Rusty's spaniel tail (below).

With a little practice, it is possible to make convincing noses, ears and really anything else that takes your fancy, although because of the time needed for the latex to set, it's a slow process and large pieces require a lot of time and patience.

Latex objects made this way begin to perish after five to ten years, faster if kept in hot, dry conditions or exposed to sunlight, but they can easily be recoated. Liquid latex reacts badly with metal, giving a grubby appearance.

Instructions for use and safety are always given on containers, but the most important thing is to work in a well-aired space because of the fumes.

Puppy play

It's easy to see how puppy play works as a submissive fantasy. Think of all the characteristics dog lovers associate with their pets; loyalty, obedience, playfulness, joy in reward and contrition in punishment. You might as well be describing the ideal submissive, while giving up your human responsibilities as a puppy takes you deeper still. Puppies are cute too, which brings it all together to make a classic submissive and exhibitionistic fantasy.

Cutie makes the perfect example. She is a French poodle owned by Sir Guy Masterleigh, who has 30 years of experience as master to ponies and puppies. Her need is to be a pet, owned and yet cared for, and to shed her cares in a way that only being in role as Cutie allows her to do. She likes to be taken for walks on her lead, as in the picture, to play fetch and beg for treats, taking pleasure in anything, which enhances her role as a puppy-girl.

An important choice for any aspiring puppy is what breed to be, which can be a strong part of

What breed of dog would you be?

the fantasy or pure practicality. Being a French poodle is ideal for Cutie, as the breed has a feminine image; small, pretty and pampered, while the traditional clip cut is instantly recognisable and means her outfit is relatively easy to make. Others prefer a full body suit in the style of their chosen breed, which might be anything or a deliberate mongrel. This part of the fantasy overlaps with furries, who are often modelled on anthropomorphic dogs,

and although they're often more comic than erotic, there are several skilled outfit makers.

Not that an outfit is essential at all. Simply being down on all fours and on a lead is enough for some, perhaps with a tail, a spiked collar or some other doggy access-ories, while black and white body paint is all you need to become a Dalmatian. Rusty, pictured, is a curly coated spaniel. Her hair comes in four pieces; a wig, two curly black extensions to make her big floppy ears and a third for her tail. Her tail, as shown, has a latex base glued to her back with

spirit gum. The ribbons help to show off her ears, but her behaviour makes her a puppy-girl every bit as much as does her outfit.

One advantage of puppy play is that you can do it indoors and that it only takes two to work properly. Accessories are also reasonably cheap and easily available. A spiked collar and chain lead from a pet shop, for example, is not only authentic but often very high quality, while you can get rubber bones, squeaky toys and even dog baskets big enough to sleep in. Just about anything designed for the larger breeds of dog will work for a human. An exception, and often a popular accessory for puppy play, is the muzzle, which needs to be custom made for the human head. These come with either metal or leather cages that cover the mouth and attach to the head in much the same way as headgear for pony-play.

There is another, very different side to the fantasy, for which "puppy play" is no longer an apt description. That is to be a wolf and hunt, what's known as the Little Red Riding Hood game, although the quarry is as likely to be male as female, there's no grandmother and when Red gets caught, the last thing the wolf is going to do is eat her, well, not in the usual way. If you take the hunting fantasy a step further and have plenty of friends to play with, it's possible to set up a full-scale hunt, with hunters, ponies, beagles and a fox.

> Then there's Little Red Riding Hood and the Big Bad Wolf.

Kitten play

Dogs have owners but cats have staff, which may be why kitten-play usually has less to do with domination and submission and more to do with sensual experience. The imagery is also quite mainstream, with its own musical, and there is a cultural perception of cats as feminine, which is perhaps why kitten-girls are commoner than kitten-boys. For the same reason, cat outfits are quite easy to get hold of and are usually quite sexy, whereas the few dog outfits that are available tend to be more comic. Yet just as with dogs, a costume isn't strictly necessary because a lot of the fantasy comes with behaviour and not with appearance.

Kitten play is ideal for those who prefer to keep their sex lives private and indoors.

For a kitten, this means lots of play and showing off, a love of attention, especially being stroked and tickled on the tummy, or, like Candi kitten in the picture, lapping up milk from a bowl. Kittens also scratch, so owners beware.

It's very much an indoor game and works well with just the two of you, so an ideal fantasy for couples who prefer to keep their sex life private.

Piggy play

Fewer people are familiar with pigs than the animals we've discussed so far, but they do fascinate many of us, which is perhaps why piggies are a lot more common than you might expect.

The perception of a pig as a dirty, fat beast and also slightly silly may not have much basis in truth, but it makes for an excellent piece of submissive imagery, so much so that when I first suggested making some piggy snouts and tails to my club I was swamped with offers to play.

My first active piggy-girl was Honey, who you can

218

see in the photo. Her nose and tail are made of latex carefully built up into shape and stuck on with gum arabic to create a realistic impression. This design is not available commercially, but you can buy piggy noses and piggy-tail butt plugs which insert directly up your bottom. Otherwise, you can make your own using liquid latex mixed in with a little pink or brown gouache to match your piggy's skin. To make the tail you need to build up an initial spiral of latex by painting a stripe onto a cone.

There's nothing a piggy likes better than a good wallow in the mud.

The neck of a Burgundy style wine bottle does very well. This then needs to be built up in the correct curly shape before attaching it to a flat, triangular plaque which can be glued onto the small of your piggy's back with spirit gum.

The nose is more complicated, and is best made by slowly building up the coloured latex on the face of a mannequin, first as a base, then a tube, which is capped by the end of the snout with its twin nostrils. It takes a lot of practice to get this right.

Feeding time can be fun too.

Piggies are really outdoor creatures, and there's nothing that they like better than a good wallow in the mud, at least in the summer. Feeding time can be fun too, especially if you invest in a zinc trough, and the "swill" needn't actually be nasty because what matters is that piggy is face down in it while you're sitting to one side eating a pasty and drinking cider, which is *de rigeur* for piggy owners, as are tweeds and wellies. Sucking a

Chewing a straw and talking in a West Country accent is optional.

straw and talking in a West Country accent is optional.

You don't need a great deal of equipment for piggy play. All she needs is her snout and tail, while a simple

switch will do for control and discipline. A lead might come in handy, but there is one fun piece of exotic equipment no owner should be without: a truffle harness.

This is similar to a pony's headgear, but in place of a bit there is a broad leather strap designed to prevent piggy eating the truffles once they've been found. The picture shows the harness laid out and being worn, with the leather cage that covers the nose and the plate that fits over the mouth, the twin straps to fasten the harness in place and the lead where it joins to a square brass fitting that lies at the back of the neck. The right hand part of the picture shows Oinky truffle-hunting in the woods to test one of the exercises for this book.

Other Animals

Anybody for worm racing?

I suppose it's possible to want to be any sort of animal, but mammals are definitely the most popular. I've seen a few bunny girls aside from the Playboy variety, two beautifully body-painted cow-girls (not the sort in tight jeans, plaid shirts, boots and hats), monkey-boys as a humiliation game for submissive men, very few sheep although it seems an obvious choice, and mice, but only in a very light-hearted way.

I've yet to come across anybody with a fish transformation fantasy, but quite a few women like the combination of helplessness and naked display that goes with being a mermaid.

Feathered costumes are popular for burlesque and giant birdcages built for girls are not uncommon, but that's really display rather than altered nature. Then there are worm races, in which submissives are bandaged from head to toe or sewn into tubular body sacks with only

their faces showing so that they can wriggle across the floor in competition for the amusement of their dominants, but again, that's not quite the same thing. What I am fairly sure of is that I have yet to experience the full range of human ingenuity when it comes to taking on animal characteristics, or to exotic sex in general. You never know what's just around the corner...

Further Exploration

This book was never intended to be comprehensive. There are a great many areas I've left out altogether, for a variety of reasons, and even for those areas I've gone into in some depth, there's plenty more to learn. If you do want to explore further, there is a wealth of information available, some good, some less so. The internet in particular is something of a minefield, almost entirely unedited and often with no more weight given to the good than the bad. Books tend to be more reliable and there are many high quality works available, especially on bondage and the deeper aspects of dominance and submission. You will also learn from each other, and if you choose to get involved with the wider scene, you'll find there's no shortage of experts ready to give guidance.

My own final piece of advice is that whoever you meet, whatever you get into, don't lose sight of what it all comes down to, sexual pleasure and fulfilment.

Exercises

1 – Making your own Victorian Splitters

If you can sew, it's easy to make your own pair of Victorian style split-seam drawers.

A – Half your maximum hip measurement + 12"

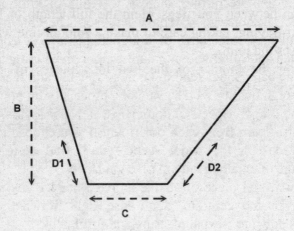

B – Waist to mid-thigh + 2"

C – Mid-thigh measurement + 4"

D – Approximately 6"

Procedure:

1 – Cut two pieces of plain linen, silk or other natural fabric to the above dimensions. The exact shape will depend on your measurements, but it should be an irregular trapezoid as shown above.

224

2 – Cut two more pieces of cloth, each 4" over your maximum hip measurement long by 6" and 4 wide respectively.

3 – On both large pieces of cloth, sew D1 to D2, creating two open cones. The seams used on a genuine Victorian 1890s bodice are done by turning the edges of the cloth under each other and sewing two parallel lines.

4 – Sewing D1 to D2 will have formed the seams which will run between your legs. Hem the full length of B to prevent fraying, taking care to make a smooth line where it crosses the join.

5 – Cut the thinner of the two long pieces of cloth lengthwise in two, join the ends to make one long length, hem the outer ends, turn it into itself until it is no more than ½" wide and sew the full length to make a neat drawer-string.

6 – Hem the ends of the remaining small piece of cloth and sew the centre of the draw-string into it just below the centre point. This will become the waistband.

7 – Sew the two main pieces together, joining the seam (above D1) at what will become the front of the drawers almost to the bottom. This joins the two A sides to make a new edge that will attach to the waistband.

8 – Overlap the two flaps that will form the rear of the drawers, doubling the cloth back to give a neat effect and fix this overlap in place with two stitches. The overlap should be around 8". *It is essential that the total length of the waist thus made exceeds the maximum hip measurement.*

9 – Double the waistband over lengthwise and sew it to the waist edge made of the two A sides, using the same seam technique as above. Take care to keep the drawstring inside and then sew up the inner edges of the waistband mouths by hand to give a neat finish.

Trim the hems with the widest, most elaborate cotton lace or *broiderie anglais* you can find, using as many layers, pleats and tucks as you please. With Victorian drawers there's no such thing as too fancy.

The result should look something like this.

2 – Making a Cane

It is simple and cheap to make your own cane, but it takes time.

1 – Buy a one-metre length of Kooboo or Dragon, *not* bamboo.
2 – Round off both ends and smooth off any rough areas.
3 – Soak it in water for at least 24 hrs.
4 – Bend the handle into a crook fix it in place with tape.
5 – Allow to dry for at least 48 hrs before removing tape.
6 – Rub in oil or wax to keep it supple.
7 – Test on a cushion dusted with talcum powder.
8 – When proficient, decide on a juicy fantasy and test your new cane on your partner's bottom.

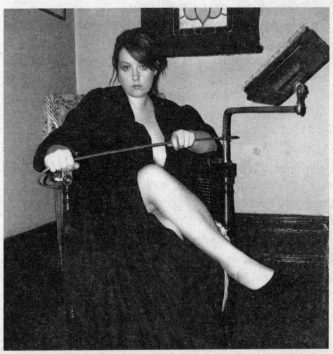

3 - Sweet Revenge – a thoroughly Wicked Game

1 – Set up your party with about a dozen kinky friends.

2 – Print Revenge Vouchers with values of ¼, ½, 1 and 5.

3 – When the party kicks off, put all your names in a hat, or girls' names in one hat and boys' in another.

4 — Take turns to draw. If somebody draws your name, he or she wins the right to top you, but you can choose what happens from a list and how exposed you're going to be.

5 – If the person take up your offer, you earn Revenge points, perhaps as follows if you've been awarded a spanking:

> ¼ points if you're spanked on your outer clothes
> ½ points if you're spanked on your underwear
> 1 point if you're spanked bare
> 5 points if you take six-of-the-best with a cane

When you have earned enough points, you can trade them in to top people who have topped you, at a value of 1 full point per session and regardless of what they did to you in the first place. If they refuse they have to take a previously agreed forfeit, which should be deeply humiliating. When you've earned enough vouchers, you can demand group forfeits or you can gang up with friends against other people, so long as the right to take revenge has been earned. Points traded in go back in the bank until earned in a fresh draw.

Once you get going, you'll realise just how subtle, and how cruel, this game can be, not just by weighing your desires and fears one against the other, but for all the opportunities it gives for scheming and deceit, alliance and betrayal, but above all, for revenge.

Age 18 and Over - For 4 to 20 Players

229

4 – Truffle Hunting

1 – First catch your pig.

2 – Equip your pig with a snout and tail, perhaps also a pair of ears. Knee pads might also be appreciated.

3 –– Choose a suitable piece of woodland with plenty of soft, mossy ground.

4 –– Purchase a reasonably large box of individually wrapped chocolate truffles.

5 – Take your pig to the woods, preferably on a warm, sunny day or there might be complaints.

6 – Piggy should be naked, or in as little as you can get away with if somebody might see.

7 – Tether piggy to a tree, either in a truffle harness or gagged and on a lead.

8 – Scent your truffles with lemon essence and hide them among the leaves. A few drops of essence per truffle should do and you might want to lay some false trails.

9 – Cut yourself a switch.

10 – Give piggy a set time to find as many truffles as possible, just by scent and crawling on all fours.

11 – Feed piggy the truffles, snuffled up from your hand.

12 – Apply your switch to piggy's bottom, at least once for every truffle missed.

13 – Recover the remaining truffles and eat.

The End

Credits

Models

Special thanks are owed to my six main models:

Ivy (*www.xivyx.co.uk*)
Joanna (*www.joannalark.com*)
Leia-Ann (*www.leiasfantasies.co.uk*)
Sophie (*www.kinky-minx.me.uk*)
Mark
Sarah

Also, many thanks to all those who helped this project come alive:

Alan, Birgit, Bryan, Cat, Chiquana, Chris, Cutie, Dagmar, Eve, Gemma, Ginny, Heather, Ishmael, Jay, Jed, Jen, Jenny, Judith, Koki, Karen, Kez, La Marquise, Laura, Liekki, Lucy, Mel, Michael, Mikki, Morphia, Nez, Peter, Robyn, Rosanna, rose, Rosie, Sep, Sev, Starry, Vicky, Victoria & Zoe.

Photography

All photographs are the copyright of Aishling Morgan unless otherwise stated.

Female Dominant picture courtesy of La Marquise
Rubber Maid picture courtesy of Robin
(*www.houseofharlot.com*)
Advanced bondage picture courtesy of Mark Varley

(www.markvarleyphoto.co.uk)
Messy Spanking picture courtesy of Bill Shipton
(www.splosh.co.uk)
Sir Guy and Cutie courtesy of Roger
(*www.adult-outdoor-pursuits.co.uk*)

Special thanks to Poetic Beauty Photography, Kacie
Kayle Photography and Karla Kissell Photography.

Artwork

Contracts picture courtesy of Sardax
- *www.sardax.com*
Lobster and Caterpillar picture courtesy of Jaden

Support

Special thanks are due to Mikki and Chris, Jason, Jen,
John, Rosie, and also:

Cosmic of London Alternative Market
(*www.londonalternativemarket.com*)
Bill Shipton of Splosh
(*www.splosh.co.uk*)
Birgit and Alan of Deadly Glamour
(*www.deadly-glamour.com*)
Graham of Affordable Leather Products
(*www.affordable-leather.co.uk*)
Heather of London Fetish Fair
(*www.londonfetishfair.co.uk*)
House of Harlot
(*www.houseofharlot.com*)
Ishmael Skyes of The Firm
(*www.the-firm.org*)

Mark Varley of Beautiful Bondage
(*www.beautifulbondage.net*)
Nick and Morphia, Violet Wands
(*www.nickandmorphia.com*)
Silken Ties
(*www.silkenties.com*)
Sir Guy Masterleigh of Tawsingham
(*www.tawse.com*)
Trainer Bryan of the North Downs' Pony Club
(*www.ndponyclub.co.uk*)
Vicky & Cat of Freak Clubwear
(*www.freakclubwear.co.uk*)

Studio Facilities

Adult Outdoor Pursuits, West Wales
(*www.adult-outdoor-pursuits.co.uk*)
Club Naughty and the Kinky Crypt
(*www.kinkycrypt.com*)
Studio 21, Chiswick
(*www.fetishist.com*)
Studio 3, Potters Bar
(www.studio-three.org)
The Barnet Bastille, Barnet
(*dungeonfurniture@hotmail.co.uk*)

HOW TO BE BAD
By Aishling Morgan

How to be Bad, 101 sexy scenes, from the romantic to the bizarre, from the inventive to the downright kinky.

Aishling Morgan suggests a broad range of delicious indulgences, picked up from personal experience and presented as a lighthearted, easy to follow guide. Whatever your tastes, you're sure to find some inspiration here!

Each suggestion comes with an easy user guide featuring romance, heat, kink and tech ratings.

£9.99

ISBN 9781907016219

For more information and great offers
please visit
www.xcitebooks.com